FILOSOFA'S REPUBLIC

FILOSOFA'S REPUBLIC

THEODORE DALRYMPLE

MIRABEAU PRESS

Published by Mirabeau Press

PO Box 4281

West Palm Beach, FL 33401

ISBN: 978-1-7357055-7-6

Second Edition

MIRABEAU

PREFACE TO A NEW EDITION

In 1984, I went to Tanzania to work as a doctor on a large construction project. This was in the heyday of President Julius K. Nyerere's 25-year rule. Known as *Mwalimu*, Teacher, he was the darling of European and North American Third-Worldists, who desperately sought both a socialist utopia that worked and an African leader whom they could admire. Nyerere fitted the bill perfectly. Seemingly modest, endowed with great personal charm, an intellectual who had imbibed Fabian socialism at Edinburgh University and had translated *Antony and Cleopatra* into Swahili, he was supposedly constructing an egalitarian rural paradise in Tanzania, combining the virtues of the simple life with the provision of modern health and educational services. Foreign countries, notably the Scandinavians, poured billions of dollars of aid into the accomplishment of this dream.

And a dream it was. The majority of the Tanzanian peasantry was compulsorily moved, or herded, from where it was living into collectivised villages. Commerce was rigorously controlled because, according to the doctrine, middlemen such as merchants were parasites and exploiters, to be excluded in favour of idealist bureaucrats of the one and only political party.

The result, predictably, was that agricultural production declined precipitously and commercial farming for crops for exchange virtually ceased. Nyerere's policy caused much unnecessary suffering and aggravated poverty. Only foreign aid kept the country from outright starvation. Corruption and favouritism flourished, and in rural Tanzania you could tell a party man by his girth. All development aid was money poured into sand. The country became ever poorer. Meanwhile, Nyerere was lauded in the West as a great thinker and economist.

The discrepancy between the image and reality, I thought, could only be captured by satire. (In those days, satire was not yet prophecy. The great development economist, Peter Bauer, used to refer to Nyerere satirically as *St. Julius*. Now Nyerere, who was a believing Catholic, is *en route* to canonisation.)

I wrote this short satire after leaving Tanzania, publishing it under the pseudonym Thursday Msigwa. Apparently, it reached Nyerere, and he asked whether Filosofa Cicero B. Nyayaya, His Excellency the Brother President of the Human Mutualist Republic of Ngombia, was supposed to be he. Indeed, it was.

If I were writing the book today, I would be a little less hard on Nyerere. He had certain virtues, or at least he lacked certain vices, by the standards of the first generation of African leaders after independence. While he was a dictator, he indulged in none of the sanguinary activities of some of his contemporaries, though his regime did not stop at mass imprisonment and murder of opponents. He was not a tribalist (a difficult thing to be in Tanzania, since there were no tribes that could have been dominant). He indulged in no great *folie de grandeur*. Eventually, he stood down.

He was fortunate in the people of his country, who were

peaceful. They were the politest people I ever knew: I cannot recall meeting a single rude Tanzanian in three years. That such politeness and good humour survived his rule suggests that it could have been worse.

INTO AFRICA

I decided to go to Africa when my daughter howled because she wanted Choco-Pops, not Frosty-Bran, for breakfast. My lecture on the value of the bran to her bowels failed to convince her. Surely, I concluded, there must be more to life than this continual domestic guerrilla warfare, more compelling dilemmas, choices of graver import.

I knew nothing of Africa, except that it was hot and poor. There is no reason why an accountant should know of anything other than tax laws and balance sheets. The advertisement for the post of financial controller of a plantation in Ngombia said that no previous tropical experience was required, only a knowledge of audits. It seemed the accounts there were in a mess, and though the plantation produced a commodity vital to the continuation of western civilisation, no-one knew whether or not it made a profit. It was rumoured that during the years of nationalisation, the plantation had avoided expropriation only by declaring a large loss.

My wife declined absolutely to accompany me because – so she said – of the presence of snakes and the absence of Culture.

I was not deterred: I thought a brief separation might make the heart grow, if not fonder, then at least less bitter.

Before I left, the company that owned the plantation, a conglomerate for whom Africa was but a hobby, thought it wise to send me on an 'orientation course', to lessen somewhat the impact of the changed circumstances in which I was about to find myself. The course was held in a Jacobean mansion in Surrey woodland, the nearest the Home Counties could come, apparently, to the African bush. It lasted four days and we learnt – between meals – about the topography, climate, ethnography, flora and fauna of our land of self-exile. One of our number was much exercised by the prospect of being eaten by Ngombians – beads of sweat appeared on his upper lip when he thought of it – and he asked every speaker whether there were still cannibals there. He would not take no for an answer.

I became friendly with a young man whom in other circumstances I should have been most unlikely to meet. It was one of those brief friendships of people thrown temporarily together. He was a newly qualified doctor who had not yet attained the portentousness of his profession. Probably he never would: he wore an unruly black beard that betrayed him at once as a rebel and an intellectual. He was unable, he said, to read of the plight of Africa without wishing to help; his conscience would not permit it. He had therefore grasped at once the opportunity offered by a charitable organisation called Suffer the Children to work in Africa for practically no salary. It was the very least he could do. And we were very fortunate, he added, to be going to Ngombia.

I asked him why he thought so.

His eyes lit up and, though he had never been to Ngombia, he spoke with fire, with passion.

"It's the one country in Africa," he said, "where the government works for the masses, not for itself."

He reeled off statistics: infant mortality rate, life expectancy, the proportion of villages with potable water, the literacy rate, the number of children vaccinated against measles. It was most impressive. I asked him how Ngombia had achieved all this.

"Simple," he said. "It's put Human Mutualism into practice."

He informed me that Human Mutualism, of which I knew little, was the political philosophy of Cicero B. Nyayaya, the first and so far only president of Ngombia.

It was, he said, a brilliant distillation of the immemorial wisdom of Africa, adapted to modern circumstances. So universally was it accepted by the Ngombian people that they had accorded their president the honorific title of *Filosofa*, the Ngijwi word for Philosopher.

Filosofa, he continued, was not as other African presidents. He did not sleep in golden beds or bathe in platinum jacuzzis. Filosofa was modest: when he went abroad, he ate only maize porridge (he took sacks of maize with him on the presidential plane). He owned no apartments in London or Paris and operated no Swiss bank accounts. This did not mean, of course, that he was unsophisticated: far from it, he had translated the whole of *Paradise Lost* into Ngijwi, the national language of Ngombia, and strangely enough it had become a bestseller there. But being a quintessential African, Filosofa believed in complete equality and simplicity. His heartfelt eloquence had moved prime ministers and peasants, churchmen and tycoons, all over the world. And no wonder: for his arguments in favour of Human Mutualism were, to any man of goodwill, virtually unanswerable.

The young doctor had brought Filosofa's books with him, which he carried conspicuously wherever he went. As a token of special esteem, he let me read them. I, he said, would understand them, unlike the other philistines in the course. And every time we met thereafter, he asked – as anxiously as if he had written them himself – whether I had read them. I replied that I had, in part, and when he asked my opinion, I said Filosofa wrote of complex matters with algebraic clarity.

"Yes," said the doctor, "it's as though scales fall from your eyes, isn't it?"

All human beings, wrote Filosofa, are equal, not in the literal sense, of course, but in the ultimate, and more real, ethical sense. According to Filosofa, Africans had always known this, until the Europeans came. Before, no man in Africa had tried to be greater than his neighbour, and in times of difficulty everyone had helped everyone else with no thought of self. It was to recapture this ancient solidarity that Filosofa devised Human Mutualism, which was neither communist nor anticommunist, but simply the expression in the African context of the highest ideals of Man, for justice, freedom, equality, democracy, etc. Man, said Filosofa, was at the centre of everything, and from now on all Ngombians were to address one another as *Brother*.

Filosofa was not against modern inventions, like the wheelbarrow, but he wanted them to benefit everyone equally. He was completely opposed, on the other hand, to exploitation: it was one of his favourite sayings that anyone who possessed more than the average man must have stolen it. Human Mutualism was to abolish exploitation forever in Ngombia, not only physically but psychologically. No-one's salary was to be more than three times anyone else's, and in his celebrated *Harisha Declaration*, that aroused enthusiasm in universities all over Europe, Filosofa laid down that no government servant should be allowed to own a shop or other business or live in a house with more than two rooms. Ngombia, he said, is a land of peasants; therefore we – the government – must live like peasants.

An organisation was required to bring about the total liberation of Ngombia from exploitation, and Filosofa founded the Party of the Mutualist Revolution. It was not an ordinary party, one among many; on the contrary, as the embodiment of the people's Mutualist aspirations, it rendered all other parties redundant, and they were therefore either abolished or absorbed. And to ensure that the party never forgot its humble roots (humility was a favourite word of Filosofa's), it was decreed that every eighth household should be represented by a party member. Not only would this representative convey to higher levels in the party the concerns of the masses, but he would also act as the Mutualist conscience of the eight households should they fail in their Mutualist duty. Above every eight such household leaders stood a party member on a higher level, above eight such members, another on a higher level still, and so on till Filosofa himself. He called this his 'Law of Eights', by means of which the party always heard the voice of the people, from whom, strictly speaking, it was indistinguishable.

The task of the party was not merely to free Ngombia from exploitation, but to lead it in its struggle for development. This did not mean, according to Filosofa, economic growth alone, or even mainly. Because Man was at the centre of everything, it was Man that had to be developed. "We should rather be poor but Mutualist," he said, "than rich but immoral." Health and education were particular concerns of Filosofa, but because Ngombia was very poor and its resources limited, it was necessary that the people be concentrated into new and much larger villages, so that schools and clinics could be provided. Of course, this meant they would have to abandon their ancestral lands; but they would soon be able to pick up elsewhere, lured by aspirin and the two times table. The party would provide them with new plots of land, at the same time ensuring that no-one ever again became an exploiter: the land would be reallocated every year by the village party Secretary, according to need and capacity.

I returned Filosofa's books to the young doctor, and he stroked them almost tenderly.

"Filosofa's one of the greatest men of this century," he said, deeply moved. "He's led his people for twenty years, he's been their guide and inspiration, yet he's so poor himself he had to ask for a loan to buy a bullock for his farm. It's wonderful to find such dedication. That's why I chose Ngombia..."

Arrival

Most cities look neat from the air. Ndinji, capital of Ngombia, is a rare exception. Favoured by nature, with a magnificent harbour on an azure sea, and with a green and fertile hinterland, it is a mess from any height or angle.

I didn't spend long there. The airport terminal was low and dark, crowded and humid. Everyone seemed in a panic, shouting, flinging his arms about, pushing, sweating profusely. No-one waited his turn. On the wall above the customs desk, at an angle, hung a picture of Filosofa, a slight man with a gap-toothed smile. A fly had somehow insinuated itself between the photograph and glass cover and had died there. Under the picture was Filosofa's title in full:

HIS EXCELLENCY THE BROTHER-PRESIDENT OF THE UNITED DEMOCRATIC HUMAN MUTUALIST REPUBLIC OF NGOMBIA FILOSOFA DR CICERO B. NYAYAYA

Across the terminal was strung a banner:

HE WHO SEEKS PERSONAL ADVANTAGE HAS NOT ACHIEVED TOTAL LIBERATION

Through the din the customs officer shouted at me:

"Have you brought presents?"

"I'm in Ngombia for the first time," I said. "I don't know anyone here." "For me," he said. "presents for me."

I stayed a night in the best hotel in Ndinji, called the Milikanjaro. It was built by the Bulgarians and looked like the headquarters of the secret police. Its grey paint was flaking as in some terrible skin disease. The lobby must always have been charmless, but now it was dangerous as well. Half the ceiling tiles had fallen or been removed, and the floor was covered in the dust of breezeblock masonry. A blackboard was posted with a notice dated three years earlier:

Dear Guest!

To Improve our Services More We are undergoing Repairings of our Beloved hotel.

Please Excuse Our inconveniences To help you better Signed management

At the reception desk a man in a stained brown jacket read Uburu (Freedom), the party newspaper. Above him was a picture of Filosofa.

"Yes," he said, scarcely looking up.

"A single room please."

"You make reservation?"

"No."

"No rooms."

This was clearly untrue, but he was deaf to my entreaties. As I watched another guest check in, I suddenly understood why. I placed a banknote on the counter, and in a single smooth movement the receptionist collected it and put it in his pocket.

"You should make reservation," he said. "Sometimes the hotel filled completely."

I wrote on the registration form, the ink spreading in spidery strands through the rough and absorbent paper.

"How long you stay?" he asked.

"One night."

"Two hundred dollars," he said, holding his hand out towards me.

"What?"

"You must pay in advance," he said. "In cash. Two hundred per cent. In dollars."

"But why?"

"Too many African delegations. Leave and no pay."

"But I'm not a member of an African delegation," I said.

"Not one law for white man and one law for African," he replied.

I asked for a porter, but they were attending a Self-Criticism meeting. Self-Criticism was one of the pillars of Human Mutualism.

"Wait half an hour," suggested the receptionist.

Impatient, however, I struggled to the lifts with my luggage. Nearby sat a party of Ngombians. Their table was cluttered with dark brown bottles of Revolution beer, mostly empty. They were noisy with hilarity, shouting jokes, slapping each other on the back and shaking hands frequently. Their faces glistened: most of them were fat. It was not quite eleven o'clock in the morning.

I called for a lift, but none came. Eventually, one of the drinking party rose and walked unsteadily towards me. His eyes were bloodshot, his speech slurred: he must have been up all night.

"Is anything wrong?" he asked. "I am the manager of this hotel."

"The lifts don't work," I said.

"No lifts between six in the morning and six in the evening," he said. "Economy measure. No foreign exchange. A problem, a big problem."

He shook his head in drunken sorrow.

"And no porters," I said. "Do you need foreign exchange for porters?"

"Ngombia is a Human Mutualist country," he said, changing his tone instantly from sorrow to self-righteousness. "We don't need porters anymore. The peasants don't have porters."

"The peasants don't have bedrooms on the seventh floor. The peasants don't pay two hundred dollars a night..."

"You don't own people if you pay them," he retorted, stiffening his back. "There is human dignity. The party selected me for hotel management..."

I left him swaying by the lift: irritation gave me renewed energy to climb the stairs.

Nothing worked in my room except the radio. There was a powerful smell of fungus and all the lightbulbs had been removed. The windows would not open because the room was airconditioned, but the airconditioner did not work. I turned on the radio and listened to the news. Filosofa had made a call to the party to be vigilant against enemies, to work harder and be more honest. And the party Secretary-General had just returned from Albania, having further cemented the indissoluble friendship between the Albanian and Ngombian peoples. He was leaving the following day for medical treatment in the United States.

I flew next morning to the plantation in a small, chartered aircraft whose pilot – a veteran of the Battle of Britain – asked me to steer as soon as we were airborne so that he could read his novel. In the early morning sun, the tin roofs of Ndinji looked like pewter. We left the city behind: the open sewers, the potholed roads, the goats and vultures grazing on garbage tips, the half-completed concrete towers rising in the midst of shanties. Soon we were flying over a wilderness, an emptiness such as we in Europe do not know. To the far horizon stretched a vast savannah, studded with acacia trees; ribbons of green snaked through the brown and parched landscape where rivers ran, their banks cool and fertile. We dipped low over the plain causing herds of wildebeest to flee and elephants to flap their ears in anger. Crocodiles slithered into the muddy waters, and bush pigs ran comically with their tails erect. I was glad I had come to Africa.

The landscape changed. Hills appeared where the trees were less stunted, creating a dense canopy of dark green over which shadows cast by small white clouds moved with silent grace. In the distance were mountains, folds of blue-green, then mauve and purple. Here and there the forest had been cleared for a village and its fields; sometimes a road ran through the forest, a long red scar of laterite. The forest seemed endless, timeless, indestructible.

The plantation was near the village of Mbaba, from which came its labourers. The centre of the village was astride a laterite road, widened into a crude plaza which in the rains was an estuary of red mud, and in the dry season deposited a fine film of red dust over everything, so that the trees looked rinsed in henna. For two hundred yards on either side of the road ran terraces of mud buildings, guest houses for passing truck drivers, or bars from which the feeble glimmer of oil lamps issued after dark. Beyond was the church, made of small rough bricks, with a tower that looked about to crumble. Next to the church was the village football pitch, uneven and pocked after the rains with tussocks of coarse grass. It served also as the parade ground of the Y.M.M., the Young Mutualist Militia, who goosestepped over it with wooden toy rifles every Thursday under the gaze of their commanding officer, the village schoolmaster. Further on still were scattered huts and a small stream, where children splashed and bathed, crossed by means of a dilapidated wooden bridge with missing planks. Throughout the village were mango trees, in whose shade men gathered to chat, and thickets of bamboo, not cultivated but growing wherever nature intended. Thin chickens pecked the ground, pigs rooted for small sustenance, threadbare dogs plagued by flies rested wherever there were shadows, and whitish ducks that looked as though they had been splashed with black ink waddled across the road, followed by ducklings. And everywhere there were children and more children, squatting by the side of the road: girls of three or four had babies strapped to their backs.

The residential quarters of the plantation were very different. Four miles away, on the edge of a thousand-foot escarpment, they gave a view of the distant mountains of which one could never tire over one's evening drink. The gardens were large and well-tended. In the season the jacarandas dusted the ground with fragrant purple blossom. The houses were neat and newly decorated: a suburb in the jungle.

I was met by Peter Smith, the plantation agronomist and my next-door neighbour. He was a tall man with a stoop; he had a fair moustache, designed I should think to disguise the weakness of his face, but only accentuating it. He was conscientious and kind, intelligent and hardworking, but not of strong character. He asked me whether I played bridge. It was, he said, the only means of escape from the social isolation of the plantation.

He introduced me to my domestic staff: the garden boy Elastic and the housegirl Athena. Elastic was digging, not very vigorously, when I arrived. He at once relieved me of my cases, for it was a poor kind of white man who carried anything for himself when there was an African at hand. The breadth of his grin gave meaning to his otherwise absurd name. Athena emerged diffidently from the house, Elastic immediately transferring the cases to her: for it was a poor kind of man who carried anything for himself when there was a woman at hand. It was weeks before Athena had the courage to look me in the eye without retiring in confusion.

I went into my house. My new life in Africa had begun.

THESIS I

Human Mutualism is not a dogma. We must adapt it to circumstances and use it creatively.

Filosofa Cicero B. Nyayaya

It did not take long to discover how things stood in Mbaba.

I soon settled into my work. The offices were a short walk away from my house. The plantation's accounts were in disarray but not beyond redemption. I was fortunate in having under my direction an exceptionally able assistant called Nero. It was only much later that I learnt something of his history: he was a former bank manager who had been caught embezzling (as are all Ngombian bank managers in the fullness of time). The shortness of his stay in gaol was a testimony to his success as an embezzler: he served only three days before buying himself out. He emerged from prison with his character unblemished in his own and his family's eyes, and probably those of society in general as well, since no less was expected of anyone in authority. Nevertheless, he thought it prudent to change his name from Innocent to Nero, the latter being an historical figure he admired, or of whom he had at least heard. He changed his surname from Mwanga to Chinga.

Nero was convinced of his own indispensability to the company, for competent men were not easy to find in Ngombia.

He was in charge of the wages department and, unaware of his record, I left him too much to his own devices. Whenever I performed a spot check everything seemed in order; until, that is, one day when I was in the General Manager's office, discussing with him our plans for expansion. A delegation of workers from the field arrived at his door.

The General Manager was a man of few words at best, and his reception of the delegation was less than friendly, for we were occupied with matters that were, as we thought, much more important. Still, it was impossible not to feel a visceral compassion for these three men, so ragged, dusty and half-starved were they. The room filled at once with the unmistakable smell of the long unwashed. They had the bearing of men who had been browbeaten all their lives, and who expected nothing else.

"Yes," said the manager, making it clear he had not much time to devote to their small concerns.

They spoke through an interpreter, for his Ngijwi was equal only to pleasantries. "They say they have come to speak to you, sir, on important business."

"Very well. What is it?"

"First they say they hope you are in full health and your family also."

The manager accepted these formal good wishes with ill-concealed impatience. "They say they are not receiving full wages, sir."

"What do you mean?"

"There is money missing, sir."

"Do they have their wage slips?" asked the manager.

He was handed some scraps of torn and crumpled paper, which reminded me inconsequentially of the half-eaten toffees I used to treasure in my pockets as a schoolboy. It was evident, however, that the men had received their wages in full. True, tax had been deducted at a ferocious rate; they had made 'contributions' to the party, the National Development Fund, the Trade Union, the Ngombian Liberation Committee for Southern Africa, and other notable causes, leaving them with pitifully little after a month's labour, but it was none of the manager's doing, and had their wages been increased their contributions would have increased likewise. The manager handed back the scraps of paper and said he was sorry, there was nothing he could do.

We expected the delegation to go, judgement having been pronounced, but they remained standing stolidly before us.

"Well," asked the manager, "what else?"

"Please, sir," replied the interpreter, who had taken the part of the men. "They say Mr Chinga has taken from their wages, please."

I had noticed that when an Ngombian became nervous, he used the word *please* inordinately.

"But they accepted and signed for their wage packets," said the manager. "But Mr Chinga, he took two hundred from each packet, please."

"How long has this been going on – allegedly?"

"Three months, please."

"Why has nothing been said before?"

"Well, please, they had an agreement with Mr Chinga. If they give him two hundred every month, please, he change their income tax so they pay less."

"And how many men took part in this agreement?"

"A hundred and sixty, please."

"So Mr Chinga has been making thirty-two thousand a month for three months?"

"Yes, please."

The manager paused for thought.

"But please," resumed the interpreter. "Mr Chinga, he doesn't keep his word. These men, they pay as much tax as before."

Now we had reached the heart of the matter. Nero had swindled them. If he had kept his side of the bargain, we should never have heard of it until he disappeared with the proceeds.

"All right," the manager told the delegation. "Wait outside."

He called Nero into his office. The black skin over Nero's plump form glistened with wellbeing.

"Good morning, sir," he said. "How are you this morning? I hope you slept well and your family..."

"Never mind that," said the manager. "Did you see those men waiting outside my door?" "Yes, sir," said Nero. "Labourers, I think."

"Exactly. They tell me you entered into an agreement with them whereby, in exchange for money every month, you would reduce their rate of tax."

Nero coughed.

"Well," asked the manager, "is it true?"

"Yes, sir," he said.

We were taken aback by the baldness of his admission. Lying, even when there was nothing to gain from it, was second nature to Ngombians, in the opinion of expatriates.

"It is true," added Nero solemnly, as if giving further information.

"How could you?" asked the manager.

He made Nero look closely at the three labourers. Their shorts and shirts were in tatters.

Their skins were dry with vitamin deficiency, flaked in a kind of crazy paving pattern. They were thin and wiry, and almost shivering. They looked at the ground.

"How could you?" repeated the manager. "You, so sleek and well-fed." Nero was not ashamed or even embarrassed.

"That is why my children are well-fed," he said. "They wouldn't be well-fed on my wages alone."

There was truth in what he said, for no Ngombian was allowed to earn more than three times the minimum, and the minimum was very little.

"But to take advantage of them like that..." said the manager, sounding less sure of himself. "You earn more in an afternoon than I do in a month," said Nero combatively.

There was truth in that, too. The manager decided to deal with the practical, rather than the moral, side of the question.

"I'll have to fire you," he said. "I have no choice."

Nero shrugged his shoulders. It was *rahati baya* – bad luck – as far as he was concerned that he had been caught.

"And we'll have to turn you over to the police," added the manager.

Nero did not seem unduly concerned; in fact, he smiled. I was incensed at this affront to our dignity. He had, for all his excuses, committed a crime and a grossly immoral act.

We sat the labourers down and asked them to write statements. Though they appeared in the national statistics as literates, this was quite beyond their powers, and their statements had to be taken by dictation. To these they put their names with unsteady hands.

I was deputed to escort Nero to the police station in the company of our security guards who wore military greatcoats that looked as though they had come down from the trenches of Flanders. The interpreter came too. The police station was scarcely more than a hut, pitch black inside even at noon, and fiercely hot. The two policemen had taken off their boots which, being uncomfortable, were for special occasions only. My unexpected visit being such an occasion, they scrambled to put them on as I entered the hut. I noticed also that the stagnant air of the tiny station was suffused with the stale fumes of exhaled alcohol. The eyes of the policemen were bloodshot as they emerged into the sunlight, and everything seemed to confuse them.

"Who is the prisoner?" they asked in Ngijwi.

Nero having been pointed out to them, they clapped a pair of handcuffs on him, but ineffectually, for the second cuff did not close and the pair merely dangled from his left wrist.

Then the policemen began to pull Nero about. They did not yet know what Nero was alleged to have done, but they were anxious to demonstrate their zeal in the service of the law, and also that they had no sympathy for wrongdoers with whom, of course, they had nothing in common. Nero accepted this rough treatment with seeming equanimity, though once – when a policeman pulled his ear – he shot me a reproachful glance, and I felt obliged to intervene on his behalf. The policemen, however, thought I was protesting at the *gentleness* of their treatment, and pulled him about some more, and even slapped him on the face.

"Don't worry, sah," said one of them, who spoke a little English. "We lock him up good, sah."

They dragged him round to the back of the police station where the village gaol was. It was but a tiny chamber of mud, with a beaten earth floor and walls that any man of average strength could have kicked down with ease. The police rented out the gaol as a guesthouse when there were no forensic inmates, and they removed the belongings of the present guest with great energy but little care. Nero was thrust on to his haunches in one corner of the cell and told not to move. The police then assured me again that he would be ill-treated.

I tried, through the interpreter, to explain what Nero had done, and I waved the depositions of the labourers about. But this was an aspect of the case that did not interest them, and they merely repeated their promise that my thirst for revenge would be satisfied.

When I went to the village next day, I was more than surprised, therefore, to find Nero sauntering at the side of the road. I stopped and got out of my car.

"Hello, sir," he said, smiling and shaking my hand vigorously.

He greeted me more as a long-lost friend than as the man who had only the previous day escorted him to prison. As far as one could tell, he harboured no resentment.

"What are you doing here?" I asked.

"I've been released," he replied jauntily. "No case to answer."

The swiftness of the legal process in Mbaba astonished me.

"You see, sir, if I was convicted, they would have to arrest all the people who had the agreement with me. They were guilty like me."

When Nero made clear to them the implications of their evidence, the witnesses refused to testify and withdrew their allegations. Nero smiled triumphantly: he had known all along it would end like this.

"So you see," he said, unable to contain his glee, "the magistrate had to dismiss the case. It wouldn't have looked very good for the company, sir, would it, if a hundred and sixty staff had been arrested?"

A few days later I heard that lack of evidence was the least of the reasons for the magistrate's dismissal of the case. He was influenced more by Nero's offer, not made wholly voluntarily, to give him half the proceeds of his little scheme.

The matter was not quite finished, however. A week later Nero appeared in my office. "Am I still fired, sir?" he asked.

He was very friendly I must say; he still appeared unresentful.

"Of course you're still fired," I said. "It goes without saying."

"But why, sir?"

"Why?"

"Yes. Why am I still fired?"

"Well, I should have thought the fact that you tried to defraud a hundred and sixty workers, to say nothing of the government, was sufficient reason."

Nero pretended to think for a moment, but he had had his answer ready from the first. "But there was no case, sir."

"I don't care what they said in court. You're guilty, you did it, you admitted it yourself..." Nero took a battered paper-covered book from his pocket.

"Under the labour laws of Ngombia, sir," he said, "you cannot fire me for a criminal act unless I have been convicted by a court of law."

He put the relevant clause before me, but I refused even to look at it.

"I don't care," I said. "You're fired anyway..."

Nero took his book and closed it neatly, almost pedantically.

"I'll go to the Union," he said. "I'll ask for reinstatement for wrongful dismissal."

There was only one union in Ngombia, called *Njata*, in effect another arm of the party.

"Do what you like," I said. "But we won't re-employ you."

"Under the labour laws of Ngombia, sir," he said, "if it is found after a union tribunal that I have been wrongly dismissed, you are legally obliged to re-instate me."

"We'll see about that," I said.

Two weeks later there was a Njata tribunal to determine whether Nero should have his job back. The chairman was a night-watchman for the company who was leader of the union and had a reputation for living beyond the means of a night-watchman. He was short, with a pot-belly and a moustache in the same style as Filosofa's. The tribunal was held in a lean-to shelter which normally housed a tractor. The chairman sat at a little wooden table, flanked by two other union representatives, a driver and a cleaner. Everyone bowed to them as they entered the shed and referred to them as *honourable members of the tribunal.*

Nero spoke on his own behalf, and all the evidence went against the company. It had dismissed him on an unsubstantiated accusation, he said, and obtained a confession 'under duress'. It was therefore clearly in breach of the Ngombian labour code, drawn up under the guidance of Filosofa himself to protect the working man and to implement the principles of Human Mutualism in places of work. Nero sat down, and I caught him winking at me, which I found offensive.

The company offered no argument in reply, and the members of the tribunal retired behind the shed to consider their verdict. Nero grinned complacently and whistled to himself. Everything had gone exactly as he could have wished. When the honourable members returned, everyone stood. The verdict was delivered by the chairman.

"We find," he said, reading from a piece of paper, "that the employee Mr Nero Chinga was correctly dismissed for misconduct from the employ of the Mbaba Estates Company, and that he has no claim whatsoever against the said company."

The smile disappeared from Nero's face. He had been certain of victory, but the cup had been dashed from his lips.

The tribunal broke up at speed, to avoid Nero's recriminations. Instead, he approached me. "I'm sorry, Nero," I said.

In spite of everything, I liked him. He was villainous only because of circumstances (I thought).

For the first time, Nero expressed anger.

"You call that justice?" he asked. "The evidence was completely on my side. It was a shut and open case. Look," he said, removing the tattered labour code from his pocket. "Look. It says here in black and white: *No employee shall be dismissed for an alleged criminal offence until such time as he has been found guilty by a properly constituted court of law.*" "Yes, it does say that," I remarked mildly.

"And have I been found guilty?" he asked.

"No, you haven't."

"Well then," he said, like a man who has just proved a geometrical theorem. "Why haven't I been reinstated?"

It was my turn to wink at him. What he did not know — what he could not have known — was that the General Manager had promised the chairman of the tribunal some window panes for the new house he was building in the village, that were available from the company but were otherwise not to be had in Ngombia, not for love or money. And all the manager asked in return was that he should write the tribunal's verdict for it, since its command of English was so poor.

THESIS II

Party leaders are dedicated to the struggle for Mutualism.
They inspire the people and have no thought for themselves.
That is why the people trust them.

Filosofa Cicero B. Nyayaya

One of the first people to visit me in my office was Mr Komba,
the village party Secretary. As such, he considered himself the
most important man in Mbaba. He liked to be friendly with
white men.

It was a hot day when he came, but he was nevertheless
kitted out as for a polar expedition. He wore a military-style
greatcoat that was several sizes too big for him and a balaclava
helmet of green wool with a bobble and *Pierre Cardin* knitted
round it in white letters. I never saw Mr Komba without this
costume, and I suspect he even went to bed in it.

He entered my room without knocking and sat down in the
chair opposite me without being asked. This was in marked
contrast to the deference all villagers had so far shown me, and
I was a little surprised to observe this by no means impressive
figure – Mr Komba was a small man, not more than five feet

29

tall, though of rapidly increasing girth – behave with such familiarity.

"I am Mr Komba," he said. "I am the party Secretary of this village. How do you do?"

He leant forward in the chair to extend his hand to me across the desk, but in so doing upset the balance of the chair and found himself sprawling over the desk. In that instant his balaclava helmet flew off his head, and I noticed that the inside was stuffed with grubby banknotes. Mr Komba snatched it back the moment he recovered.

"Sorry for that, sir," he said, upright once more. "I hope you'll overlook."

"Overlook what, Mr Komba?" I asked, thinking he referred to his stash of banknotes. "I did a mistake. I fell over. I didn't mean to disturb."

His little accident had sapped Mr Komba of his confidence, and he became so abjectly obsequious that I felt very uncomfortable. In the respect shown me by the other villagers there was an attractive element of shyness, but in that of Mr Komba there was only the toadying of a small-town shopkeeper faced suddenly with a titled customer.

"Please say nothing more about it, Mr Komba," I said. "Now, is there anything I can do for you?"

He said he had come only to introduce himself, that he wanted nothing, but it was the duty of the party Secretary to welcome newcomers to the village in the spirit of Human Mutualism. I thanked him for his kindness and told him, somewhat against my inclination, that he would be welcome in my office any time. For the company's sake, I thought it wise to cultivate him. I went so far as to offer him a cup of coffee.

He leant forward again, but carefully this time. "I'd prefer beer," he said confidentially.

I said I was sorry, we did not drink in the office, certainly not before lunchtime; and Mr Komba, disappointed, said all right, he would have a cup of coffee then, as though he were making a generous concession. He took the cup and shovelled eight spoons of sugar into it with demonic speed (sugar, like everything else, was a rare commodity in Mbaba). It did not all dissolve and when he finished the coffee he ate the sugary sludge at the bottom of the cup with enormous relish, smacking his lips so vigorously that the bobble on the top of his balaclava vibrated.

"You like sugar?" I asked him when he had finished.

"Yes," he said, scraping the bottom of the cup with the spoon. "But it is difficult to find these days."

"Why is that?" I asked.

"Speculators, hoarders, black marketeers, economic saboteurs," he replied. "The imperialists are trying to destroy Human Mutualism. That is why we have to pay three hundred and fifty for a kilo of sugar when the government price is thirty. And they put stones in the sugar to make it weigh more heavier."

"Are you sure you are not mistaking cause for effect?"

Mr Komba did not stay for a discussion but promised to return soon. He was as good as his word: a fly could not have been more assiduous in its attendance at a dungheap than Mr Komba at our office. His appetite for small favours was insatiable, and whenever he was granted one, according to Christopher, my clerk, he went boasting in the village that the company needed him, that he was indispensable to it. He held aloft in the bar that evening whatever small item he had managed to extract, as tangible proof of his power and influence. He was at pains to point out that no-one else in the village was treated with such consideration by the company.

It was true we did not want to upset him. In small things, such as rights of way and extension of our land by a few acres, he was quite powerful. To the villagers, however, he was all-powerful. It fell to him, as the embodiment of the people's will, to redistribute the village land each year, private ownership in land having been declared by Filosofa to be incompatible with the principles of Human Mutualism. There were rich pickings for Mr Komba.

Every week, after church, there was a village meeting held under the direction of the party which everyone was expected to attend. Failure to do so was interpreted as individualism verging on anti-Mutualism. People gathered round the football pitch, the lucky ones finding a place in the shade of a tree. When everyone was in his place and none was missing, Mr Komba sent word that he was now approaching. The villagers, on receiving this message, set up a rhythmical clapping, the women ululated a cry of greeting, and then everyone started to chant:

"He's coming, he's coming, our leader is coming!"

Mr Komba would arrive, still in his greatcoat and balaclava, and wave deprecatingly to the crowd. He would make a speech, taking Human Mutualism as his theme, and then start a discussion on village matters. Everyone was allowed to participate in this, though in fact everything had been decided beforehand, by competitive tender for Mr

Komba's favour, as it were. During these pointless discussions Mr Komba would reiterate over and over again that Ngombia was a democracy, in which everyone could have his opinion.

One day Mr Komba appeared at my office in a state of agitation. He evidently had an urgent request to make, and I went at once to the crux of the matter.

"What is it that you want, Mr Komba?"

"I have a problem, sir, a big problem," he said, sinking as though exhausted by care into the chair opposite mine.

"What kind of problem, Mr Komba?"

"A medical problem, sir. It is serious."

"Why come to me, then? I'm not a doctor. You should go to the village dispensary."

I knew that Mr Komba would rather die than be seen waiting for the rural health aide to attend him.

"I need medicine, sir."

"All the more reason to go to the dispensary," I said.

"Not that kind of medicine, sir."

"What kind of medicine then, Mr Komba?"

"After shave lotion."

I confess I laughed. People think wealth breeds a taste for luxury; so does poverty, only more so.

"After shave lotion is not medicine, Mr Komba."

"It is good for the skin, sir."

"I doubt it."

"I need it very badly, sir."

I learnt later that the magistrate, Mr Komba's deadly rival for power in the village, had somehow procured a bottle. It became essential for the preservation of Mr Komba's prestige that he, too, should obtain one.

It so happened that we needed Mr Komba's cooperation at that time for our plan to irrigate some of our fields, using water from the stream that ran through Mbaba. I therefore found him a bottle, and he was so grateful that he offered to pay for it. I said it was not necessary.

Mr Komba put this bottle to maximum use. At one of the village meetings, he held it up as proof of the party's power, and also of the correctness of its policies. If the villagers would only follow the party's directions, he said, one day everyone would have a bottle of after shave lotion. Of course, Mr Komba was drunk at the time.

Although the party prided itself on its revolutionary credentials, and totally rejected the humiliations of the past, Mr Komba lost no opportunity to associate himself with the company and its white staff, who lived in all but colonial style. The more he was seen in their company (he thought), the greater his prestige in the village. And therefore almost every time we drove out of our neat little suburb, we would find Mr Komba at the side of the road, flagging us down for a lift.

"Where are you going?" we would ask.

"Where are you going?" Mr Komba would reply.

And on being informed of our destination, Mr Komba would exclaim with delight: "A coincidence! That's exactly where I'm going."

Then he would climb happily into the car. As we passed someone in the road or through the village, he bestowed a regal wave through the window. The villagers stared at him as they stared at any vehicle that passed. It seemed these moments of triumph amply repaid his hours of waiting by the roadside, and the long trudge home afterwards.

But it was when the village was visited by some important party dignitary or functionary that Mr Komba attained his maximum glory. Naturally, such visits were few and far between, for Mbaba was isolated and insignificant; and so Mr Komba needed all the more to prove to the member of the Central Committee or government minister his total devotion to the cause of Human Mutualism, in the hope of promotion to a more senior, and lucrative, post.

Therefore, no-one could have been more diligent than Mr Komba in preparing welcomes for distinguished visitors; he spared no effort, his own or other people's, in ensuring their success.

Some months after my arrival in Ngombia it was announced that the Secretary-General of the party, Brother Hashmi Kabawa, was to visit Mbaba. His purpose was not clear, except that the hierarchy thought it necessary to show itself from time to time to the people. But whatever the purpose, Mr Komba busied himself as never before with preparations for this historic event.

As usual, his first call was on us at the plantation: he requested assistance with transport, a public address system, portable generators, gin, materials for posters and banners, sugar, lights, musical instruments, whisky, money, beer, fuel and other items necessary for welcoming such a visitor. Six of our vehicles were commandeered for three days before, and two days after, the visit; rage inwardly as we might at such an imposition, we knew it was a condition of permission to trade in Ngombia at all.

Mr Komba toured the surrounding villages and informed them of the voluntary contributions they were each to make towards the success of the forthcoming event. Each of them was to collect ten sacks of maize and five of beans, without fail. When the villagers protested, Mr Komba grew angry at their ingratitude for all the favours shown them in the past by the party; and he reminded them that Mbaba, of which he was party Secretary, was the distribution point for all the goods (few enough) that reached them. The villagers understood and surrendered.

For several weeks before the Secretary-General's visit, Mbaba was the scene of unprecedented activity. Some of the more conspicuous potholes were filled in and smoothed over with hard-drying mud, the area round the houses was swept daily, by order; streamers bearing militantly Mutualist slogans were tied between trees; a pedestrian crossing in black and white was painted across the road, though it soon disappeared under the dust and had to be repainted several times, creating a terrible mess; and drains were dug for the first time in the village's history. Most surprising of all, the village shop, which had always been almost empty, filled two days before the visit with merchandise such as soap, sugar, bales of cotton prints, and even toothpaste, though of course the villagers were not allowed to buy any of it. For this was the stock that preceded the Secretary-General and his retinue wherever he went, to create the impression of general prosperity and contentment.

The historic day arrived. A small stand had been built at one end of the football pitch in which the important people of the village, of whom I was one, were to rub shoulders with the dignitaries. The rest of the villagers were to gather round the pitch or line the route along which the cavalcade was to pass. For several days beforehand Mr Komba had given them lessons in waving; and a few hours before the scheduled arrival the village policemen shooed the stragglers from their huts and gave them a quick revision course on traditional welcomes with their boots and truncheons.

Mr Komba took up his position in the middle of the pitch. He was elated, but nervous too. The visit was a great opportunity, but there were correspondingly great dangers. He repeatedly looked round to check that everything was in order, he could hardly keep still, and gave one the impression he was standing in a nest of biting ants. Behind him was a troupe of dancers, specially formed for the occasion, with bouquets of empty cans tied round their ankles for percussive effect. They each wore a special tee-shirt, with a slogan painted in a circle round the party emblem:

MBABA WELCOMES HISTORIC VISIT OF HONOURABLE PARTY SECRETARY HIS EXCELLENCY BROTHER HASHMI KABAWA

The tee-shirts were Mr Komba's own idea, of which he was especially proud. When the Secretary-General learnt how hard it had been to get them, how he had laboured for weeks to find them, surely Mr Komba would be in line for swift promotion?

The cavalcade began to arrive at last, two hours late. There were thirty vehicles or more, raising clouds of dust visible from far off. Mr Komba strained his eyes for the white Mercedes in which Hashmi Kabawa always travelled, but it was not to be seen. The women ululated and the men clapped, as they had been told, but Mr Komba looked anxious. Eventually one of the vehicles, a Land Rover, drew up beside him and he rushed forward to open the door. A man in dark glasses, a well-pressed safari suit, with a large paunch which preceded him, levered himself out awkwardly. It was not the Secretary-General, who had been taken ill again and had flown once more to America for further treatment, but the Director of the Institute of African Ideology in Ndinji. This was something of a disappointment, for the banners strung across the road all alluded to the Secretary-General's genius; and it was particularly disappointing to Mr Komba, for whom an acquaintance with the Secretary- General, however fleeting, would have been an invaluable upward step. Still, the Director of the Institute of African Ideology, while not in the white Mercedes class, was important enough; and so the welcoming ceremony had to go on.

After the Director and his entourage of about fifty had watched the dancers for a few minutes, during which they showed signs of impatience – for the dancing was primitive – they trooped off into the stand, which quivered under their weight and looked about to disintegrate, though fortunately for Mr Komba it held.

First came the march-past of the schoolchildren. They had been taught to goosestep by the teacher, but not with sufficient precision, for some of them received intermittent kicks from behind. They were small and ill-fed, and the march went slowly. They clutched their toy weaponry to their chests, and looked terrified as they passed the stand. The guests laughed and pointed to the children who made mistakes.

Then the Director of the Institute of African Ideology addressed the assembled villagers. He thanked them for coming, and said their presence was yet another affirmation of the commitment of the Ngombian people to the building of

Human Mutualism. Human Mutualism, he continued, was creating a totally New Kind of Man (at this, Mr Komba applauded, and signalled the villagers to do likewise). It was thanks to the wise leadership of Filosofa, said the Director, that the principles of Human Mutualism were now government policy, as laid down in the Harisha Declaration (Mr Komba signalled the women to ululate). But he would be less than honest, continued the Director, if he did not admit that certain activities continued in Ngombia that were incompatible with Human Mutualism. For instance, while some people went hungry, others used their surplus maize to brew beer. (The villagers, who by now had got into the rhythm of the thing, applauded again, until Mr Komba's look of horror cut them short.) This was not Human Mutualism, said the Director, but its very opposite. He appealed to the villagers to grow more food and to share their surplus with their less fortunate neighbours by selling it to the National Maize Corporation, in accordance with old Ngombian traditions of solidarity.

He spoke in the blazing sun for nearly an hour and a half, but I do not recall that he said more than this. All Ngombians possess a talent for prolonging what they have to say, and even regard it as rude to express themselves as tersely as possible, Human Mutualists more than most. The villagers stood patiently: they were used to waiting.

When the Director had finished, Mr Komba thanked him and the other party leaders effusively for having taken the trouble to come to Mbaba, which would remember this day for all time, and he thanked them also not only for the inestimable benefits they had bestowed upon Mbaba, but for those they had bestowed upon the country as a whole, and he was speaking not just for himself, but from the hearts of all the villagers, who, as a small token of their gratitude, had collected some produce which Mr Komba hoped the Director would be good enough to accept on the party's behalf. Mr Komba gave a signal and a group of men waiting at the side of the stand carried heavy sacks of maize and beans which they laid on the ground at the feet of the Director, who in turn signalled that they should be counted and loaded on to the Land Rover.

Mr Komba hoped the dignitaries would join the feast afterwards, but they pleaded pressing business elsewhere, and departed abruptly with the crates of *Revolution* beer they had brought with them. The villagers dispersed.

The goods in the shop disappeared overnight, and the pedestrian crossing was trodden into the dust. The banners and other decorations, on the other hand, were left to wither away of their own accord. When I saw him next day, Mr Komba was disconsolate and considerably depressed.

"What is the matter, Mr Komba?" I asked. "I thought the visit went very well."

"I am ruined," he said. "I am finished completely."

"But why?"

Mr Komba explained that before he left Mbaba, the Director told him he considered the gifts collected by the villagers totally inadequate for such a visit, and that fifty people had a right to expect more for the effort of coming all the way from Ndinji. It therefore fell to Mr Komba to collect further gifts for despatch to the capital. And it was well-known that if you wanted one sack of anything to reach Ndinji, you had to send at least two.

So Mr Komba set about his task, and the people grumbled

and resisted passively, but in the end complied with his demands, reinforced as they were by his threats. And he, having no-one in the village to whom he could confide his troubles, used to come to me to lament the hardships of a leader's life. The people were ignorant, he said, and did not understand the aims of the party; nor did they understand the difficulties under which a leader like him was expected to work, and by the way, could I let him have a tube of toothpaste?

The disastrous visit notwithstanding, Mr Komba got his promotion. He was appointed party Secretary of a small town in another part of the country, much larger than Mbaba, that offered him a wider field of action. Elated by the news, he decided to hold a farewell feast for himself, to which he invited all the villagers. I too was invited, but I chose not to be too closely associated with Mr Komba and therefore quickly invented a prior engagement.

For several days before the farewell feast, his entire household was busy in preparation. Goats, chickens, pigs and even a cow were to be slaughtered: the villagers ate meat but rarely, and such a surfeit was without precedent. There were mounds of rice the size of anthills; cauldrons of maize porridge; vats of potatoes and boiled vegetables. And of course there was an ocean of maize beer.

The feast was to be held in the mud-brick go-down of the National Maize Corporation, in which the peasants were supposed officially to store their surplus maize. Naturally, it was empty and even the rats had given up waiting.

Mr Komba paid for the feast from his own pocket, much to everyone's surprise. Such a thing had never been known before. Of course, everyone knew where the money came from in the first place, and some said the feast was an admission of guilt, others a form of boasting. But everyone in the village watched the preparations closely.

On the night of the feast, I went to bed early, but at just past midnight I became vaguely aware of a tapping at my window. At first, I incorporated it into my dream; it must have been several minutes before I realised there was someone outside.

It was Mr Komba. He was wearing the same clothes, but they were dishevelled, and he was distraught. He looked like a man who had been through a violent storm, though the night was fine.

"Come quickly, sir," he said. "Please come quickly!"

"Why? What's the matter?"

My head was still heavy with sleep and images of disaster formed slowly in my mind. "Just come, please, please!"

I dressed and drove Mr Komba through the blackness of the village. He had walked to my house and would not disclose the purpose of his coming. Normally he had difficulty in remaining silent: tonight, however, he said nothing. He was like a man in pain.

We reached the go-down. It was filled with a guttering, shadowy, reddish light and a faint smell of paraffin. Strung across the roof were faded Christmas decorations and even a few balloons. At the far end of the go-down were the containers of food and drink, watched over by his wife and children. I have never seen so much food gathered in one place. But otherwise, the go-down was completely empty. There was not a villager in sight.

"Where are they all?" I asked.

"They have not come," said Mr Komba. "I have went to all their houses, but they say they will not come to my feast. I ask them, I reason with them, I order them, but still they will not come. I have prepared all this food. What will I do?"

He swept his arm round the go-down. Tears almost started in his eyes.

He had scoured the village seeking guests to eat his food. He had tramped through fields, crossed the stream, fallen into ditches. His search, however, had been in vain, the villagers were united and would not come, despite the meat. He was humiliated in the eyes of his family, who stood watching him from among the vessels of food.

"Can't you order your workers to come?" he asked.

I said it was nearly one o'clock and they had to go to work at daybreak. Besides, I had no such power: Ngombia was a free country.

Mr Komba, crushed, begged me at least to take a little food. I had eaten already, but I could hardly refuse. On a dented metal plate Mr Komba piled glutinous rice and some greasy, cold goat stew, and a tough and fibrous chicken leg. He put a little food on a plate for himself but had no appetite to eat it.

Altogether, it was the most melancholy meal I have ever eaten. It taught me that, under certain unusual circumstances, even a Human Mutualist can be human.

THESIS III

Justice is not only a matter of punishing the guilty. Without equality there can be no justice.

Filosofa Cicero B. Nyayaya

Mr Komba warned me against his rival, Mr Brown the magistrate. The mere fact he had taken a European name, though he was no more European than any other villager, was a clear sign he was getting above himself and was filled with ambition. I must watch him closely, Mr Komba said, and deal with him severely. He was a big thief, a villain; above all, he was as unreliable as a snake.

I dealt with Mr Brown severely, but with consequences I had not foreseen.

Mr Brown was very unpopular in the village and my clerk, Christopher, lost no opportunity to enumerate his faults.

"Brown very bad man," he said one day, with somewhat theatrical emphasis, the subject of law having arisen in passing.

"In what way, Christopher?" I asked.

"Brown, he drink ten bottles of beer every night," he said.

"He like beer too much."

Beer was rarely seen in Mbaba, and when it was, it commanded a very high price. Only the army had a constant supply, and at a concessionary price.

"Brown, he earn no more than me, so where he get the money for beer?"

It was not difficult to imagine the source of Mr Brown's additional income.

"Every night beer, every night beer," said Christopher, shaking his head sadly.

"What do you expect, Christopher?" I asked. "Everyone here takes bribes."

"But Brown, he very bad man. Very bad."

Christopher paused, as though there were something obscene he couldn't quite bring himself to say.

"Yes?" I said to encourage him.

"He take your money," he said at length. "And then he send you to prison same-same as if you no pay."

In other words, Mr Brown took bribes but failed to act upon them: he overturned all notions of justice.

I asked Christopher why, if Brown did not act on bribes, people still offered them. He replied that Brown *sometimes* took notice of them: often enough to make it still worthwhile to try. But there was no certainty: it all depended.

"On what?" I asked.

Christopher said he didn't know. "On size, I should think," I said.

According to Christopher, the whole village was afraid of Mr Brown. It was not only his appetite for beer that was insatiable, but for young women and girls as well. If an accused had an attractive wife or daughter (and almost every wife or daughter was attractive to Mr Brown), private access to her was the only bribe he would accept. If such a bribe were refused, he would mete out a savage sentence, even for a trivial offence. Before long, his hold over the village was so strong that the mere threat of arrest for some imaginary crime was enough to make men deliver up their wives or daughters to him for as long as he pleased. Mr Brown was about sixty.

It was no use the villagers complaining about him: he had *connections*. He had been a member of the party since its foundation, though his name was different then. He was a *Hero of Independence*, with a medal, that is to say, he had once made a speech under the eyes of the colonial police. The villagers could say nothing against Mr Brown, therefore, and their only recourse was to magic. Every week since his arrival in Mbaba, headless kittens, dead rats, bouquets of magical herbs and daubs of mud and blood appeared outside his house, planted in the dead of night. But Brown was the only Ngombian I ever met who was a genuine unbeliever in the power of magic, and he laughed at these feeble attempts to kill him. He just kicked them out of his way. But they frightened his wives, and eventually they ran away; which, of course, did little to reduce Mr Brown's appetite for the young women of the village.

But the worst thing about Brown – from the point of view of the company – was his persistent refusal to find any of our employees guilty of theft, when they had been caught not red but crimson handed. For instance, a worker of ours was apprehended in possession of parts of an hydraulic pump, of a kind not to be found within a radius of two hundred miles, and the company was able to show, moreover, that those very parts were missing from its pump. But Mr Brown dismissed the case because, he said, it had not been proved *beyond reasonable doubt* that the parts in question belonged to the company's pump.

There were many such cases, and we knew that his refusal to convict was not merely coincidental. The General Manager believed that, as a Hero of Independence, Mr Brown wished to disoblige those whom he considered colonial leftovers.

"They're very sensitive about that kind of thing," he said. "The officials, I mean, not the ordinary people."

I was uncertain this was the correct explanation. It was generally known in the village – how could it not have been – that the plantation's foreign employees had access to certain goods, free of duty, like whisky, tea and shampoo, that were deemed essential to their welfare, and that were otherwise unobtainable in Ngombia. They were craved, therefore, with passionate longing by the villagers: in Mbaba, a packet of tea bags was caviare and champagne rolled into one. But never once had any expatriate employee of the company offered to share the fruits of this privilege with Mr Brown who, as a big man in the village, would have expected it. And from his disappointment, I surmised, grew his refusal to convict our thieves.

I had soon an opportunity to test my theory. It was a time of particularly acute shortages, when the village shop was emptier than usual. Mr Brown appeared in person at my office and asked to see me. He wore a safari suit, a sure sign of importance in Ngombia, though it was ill-fitting and stained with the thousand residues of village life. His hair was flecked with white curls, and he carried his stomach like a pregnant woman. The unaccustomed exertion of walking had made his face glisten.

"Good morning, sir," he said, mopping his brow. "I am Mr Brown, the magistrate of this village."

I said I was pleased to meet him, I had heard much about him. He seemed strangely diffident for a Hero of Independence: was it habit or tactic?

I asked him what I could do for him.

"I need your help, sir," he replied. "I am in trouble, deep serious trouble."

I didn't know whether I could, or wanted to, help him, but I asked him what he needed.

"You see, sir, I cannot try my cases. That is very serious. Think of law and order. It is very dangerous."

"Why can't you try your cases?" I asked.

"No pens, no paper."

I covered my mouth with my hand to conceal my smile. I asked him to go on.

"So I cannot write reports to headquarters. They keep asking for them, but I cannot write them, sir. I cannot reply even to their letters. And now they have written to me, sir, telling me that unless I send my reports within ten days, I will be disciplined..."

I mentioned the general belief he had contacts in high places. Could not they help?

"But how can I reach them, sir? It will be too late. I have enemies at district headquarters, and they will be happy to destroy me." He paused. "Everyone has enemies," he added.

I enjoyed watching Mr Brown, amorous magistrate, conqueror of village wives, squirming before me. It appeared

I had his fate in my hands. Righteous indignation is the most beguiling of emotions.

"So?" I asked.

"So I need paper and pens, sir."

"Are there none in the village, in Mbaba Mutualist Cooperative Store, for example?"

"Completely none," he said, stretching his arms out wide to indicate finality.

"And what about Ongea?" I asked. "Can't you get some there?" (Ongea was the nearest town.)

"Completely none there too," he replied.

"Well, I suppose I could let you have some..."

I made it sound like a matter of complex calculation.

"Please sir..."

He wrung his hands, his fingers writhing like snakes.

"But of course," I said, "I expect something in return."

"What is it, sir? I'll do my best."

"Well, since I arrived in Mbaba, a lot of our workers have been caught stealing..."

Mr Brown tutted furiously and said that stealing was a problem nowadays in Ngombia, a big problem.

"...and strangely enough not one of them has been convicted in your court, though many were found with the stolen goods in their possession. The impression has naturally been created that it is possible for workers to steal from the company with complete impunity, a most unfortunate impression, I think you'll agree, from the company's point of view."

"There was no evidence, sir," said Mr Brown, referring to the latest such case. "Under Ngombian law there must be evidence..."

"And I hear from certain quarters in the village, Mr Brown" (from Christopher, actually) "that some of the stolen property finds its way into your possession, notably a portable generator and a..."

Mr Brown laughed a hollow laugh.

"Gossipings, sir. You mustn't listen to gossipings. People will say anything about officers of the law. They are not popular in any country."

"But to return to your little problem, Mr Brown. I think you said you needed pens and paper urgently?"

"Maximum urgently," he said.

"Well, the company will give you what you need but on one condition."

"What is that, sir? I will do my best."

"That from now on, you send our thieves to prison for at least a year."

"That is easy, no problem, sir."

"And we don't want to hear any more of this nonsense about no evidence. When we say a man's a thief, he's a thief."

"I understand, sir. When you say a man is a thief, I send him to lock-up."

"Exactly."

Mr Brown looked at his feet. He was crushed: his judicial independence had been taken from him, and only for pens and paper. I felt no pity for him, however, but thought he would be more loyal if he were left with a little of his dignity.

"Do you like whisky, Mr Brown?" I asked. "Oh yes, sir," he said, brightening.

It was not so much that anyone in Ngombia liked whisky, it

was more that if you were seen drinking it you were known at once as a person of consequence. And to own a whole bottle...

"You can have a bottle a month on the same terms. Thank you, sir."

He had not sold himself so cheap, then, and he regained a little confidence. I called the office boy to give Mr Brown two pens and a sheaf of paper.

"When you need more," I said, "just ask."

This arrangement, I thought, would more likely remind him of his obligation to the company. "Thank you, sir."

The office boy returned with the pens and paper, which I gave to Mr Brown. Far from expressing delight, as I had expected, he drew back horrified.

"What's the matter?" I asked.

"I cannot use those pens, sir," he said.

"Why not? Look, they work..." I scribbled across a page to demonstrate.

"But they are green, sir."

I thought it odd that he should express, at this late stage, so fastidious an aesthetic preference.

"Yes," I said, "I agree it's not a very nice colour, but it so happens we have a lot of green pens in stock."

"But green is the party colour, sir," said Mr Brown, still horrified.

I failed to see the significance of this. Mr Brown explained.

"Only one man in the country is allowed to use a green pen on official papers, sir."

I understood: it was not difficult to guess who that one man might be. There was only one man in Ngombia: Filosofa. I called the office boy to change the colour of Mr Brown's pens.

"And not red," said Mr Brown. "Only the secret police use red."

After my interview with Mr Brown, there was a decline in the amount of company property that went missing. He was as good as his word, or even better, for he began to sentence our thieves to five years' hard labour, having first subjected them to a lecture on the virtue of honesty. Once, when he had not fully recovered from his nocturnal communion with his monthly bottle of Scotch, he mistook a witness for the prisoner and sentenced him to four years. It was only with the greatest difficulty that Mr Brown was induced to see his error, and even then insisted the witness should serve his term, on the ground that all Ngombians were thieves. An adjournment was called, not by the sound of Mr Brown's gavel, which he struck on anything or anybody that came within range, but by the melting away from court of everyone connected with the case, the prisoner included, while Mr Brown fell into a stertorous slumber.

Nevertheless, the new system worked well, even if the sentences were a trifle severe. A single night in an Ngombian gaol, I was told, was not an experience lightly to be dismissed. The sensation of rats running over one's face is not easily forgotten. But I felt I had done my best for the company and had not subverted the course of justice, for there was no justice in Ngombia to subvert.

Sometime after the institution of the new regime at the magistrate's court, Christopher entered my office and hovered around my desk.

"Henry Muhema not guilty, sir," he said after a time. "What was that, Christopher?" I asked, looking up. "Henry

Muhema not guilty, sir."

Henry Muhema was the foreman of our workshop who had been arrested a few days earlier when various pieces of equipment that had been reported missing were found in his locker. I was surprised to learn this, for Henry Muhema had worked many years for the company with an unblemished record. He was a deeply religious man who tried actually to live by his beliefs. At lunchtime he studied the Bible, he never drank, and most remarkable of all he put aside a tenth of his wages – small as they were – to help people poorer than himself. He was an upright man in circumstances that made it almost impossible. And now he had been shown to be a rogue like the others.

"What do you mean, Christopher?" I asked.

"I mean Henry Muhema, he not steal all those things."

Christopher told me that some of the men under Henry Muhema in the workshop had planted the allegedly stolen goods in his locker. It was they who reported him to the authorities.

"But why, Christopher? Henry was a nice man, always polite and friendly..."

"Very polite man," he said.

"To everybody."

"To everybody, sir."

"And a good man, Christopher. He gave money to the poor."

"A very good man, sir."

"Then why would anyone..."

Christopher laughed for a moment and shook his head.

"This is Ngombia, sir, this is Ngombia. Money speaking,

only money speaking."

"I don't know what you mean, Christopher. Explain yourself."

He explained. Filipo Wanza, Henry's deputy in the workshop, coveted his position as foreman, and since there was no prospect in the ordinary way of his promotion, he promised to share the increase in his wages with the men who framed Henry.

And Brown, now all zeal and efficiency, had "made an example", as he called it, of Henry Muhema because he was a dangerous character, a snake in a dik-dik's skin. He sentenced him to seven years. Henry Muhema was taken away to prison, no-one knew where, and it was impossible to trace him.

I went to see Mr Brown about the case. But he was drunk, and all he would or could say was, A dangerous man, a very dangerous man.

Was it my fault? Filipo Wanza was appointed foreman in Henry Muhema's place. His wage increased by a pound a week, divided between five.

Thesis IV

Under Human Mutualism there will be no wealth and no poverty. All social distinctions will cease.

Filosofa Cicero B. Nyayaya

There was fear in the village, of Komba and Brown, fire, drought, illness and strangers, but especially of the supernatural. Spirits were everywhere, and magic caused all untoward events. But the terrors of the villagers were so woven into the fabric of their lives that they lived perfectly happily with them – as, indeed, they lived with poverty.

And so at first my interest in the natural world about me seemed to them in some way sinister: a search, perhaps, for objects of magical power. They, who had lived nowhere else, could not conceive that to me everything was so exotic, that nature here was so profligate and flamboyant that even my accountant's soul was stirred. The birds were not the drab little brown and grey creatures of an English suburban garden, but chattering, cavorting exhibitionists, showing off their scarlet or golden or sheeny blue feathers to the world, or trailing their two-feet-long tail feathers in playful, teasing flights. Even the crows were handsomely pied. And the insects were astonishing. There were bees and moths the size of small birds, and brilliant grasshoppers with crimson, blue and yellow striped legs. The butterflies were tantalisingly iridescent. The moths that gathered round the porch at night, attracted by the light, were infinite in shape and form and colour, some of horror-film hairiness, others of such lace-like delicacy that it seemed a breath of air must destroy them. Great winged beetles crashed against the windows and fell to earth, their shiny black carapaces heaped into warrior's horns and lances. Ants an inch long marched up the whitewash, while even the slugs that slimed their way across the paths were brilliant canary yellow.

Eventually the villagers accepted that my fascination with these everyday creatures was harmless; indeed, it confirmed what they had always known, that the white man, though powerful and intelligent, was quite mad. And nothing confirmed it more certainly than my interest in frogs. In England a frog is a retiring and camouflaged creature, but in Mbaba, after the first rains had fallen, a multitude of amphibians emerged from I know not where, and even entered the houses. There were bloated bullfrogs, complacent as self-made men, frogs with bright yellow stripes down their backs that fled by the hundred as one approached and jumped with a plop into deep puddles; and tiny jewelled tree frogs, their delicate fingers expanded at their ends into little suction pads. There were snow-white frogs that turned black when handled; two-tone frogs of grey and red; golden, orange, and lime-green frogs that leapt half as high as a man. How amusing the Africans found my delight in these creatures they took so much for granted!

I liked the lizards too, from the translucent and faintly pink geckos that cleared the walls of flies, to the monitor lizard, five feet long, that slunk guiltily away through the undergrowth when disturbed. Most startling of all were the skinks with sky-blue heads and orange tails, that looked as though they had rolled themselves in a barmaid's makeup. They ran too fast to catch and scuttled up trees.

But I had no difficulty at all in catching chameleons that rested on the lower branches of trees or sluggishly crossed the road. Even in an emergency, they did not accelerate: they rocked back and forth indecisively, as though unable to make up their minds which way to go, their turret eyes swivelling lugubriously in all directions at once and finding the world no good wherever they looked. When held, they turned their heads slowly and opened wide their jaws, emitting a sound like the scream of someone with laryngitis. They would have looked fearsome, if only they had been a thousand times bigger. As it was, they soon resigned themselves to captivity and obligingly changed colour for the amusement of their captor.

One day I caught a chameleon just outside our office and, thinking to demonstrate the marvellous delicacy of its construction to my incurious African staff, took it with me inside. The cashier's room was guarded by a sentry with an ancient rifle, more dangerous to the firer than the fired-upon, but when he saw the emerald reptile clinging to my forearm, he threw down his weapon and fled. The reaction of the clerks was the same: they abandoned their pens, slid from their chairs and backed away. Abject terror was written on their faces.

I went to the cashier, the most educated man in my office. He had been to university and had seen Europe. Surely he was not afraid?

He was hard at work when I entered. Glancing up, he saw the chameleon. He rose from his chair and slipped round to the far side of his desk, keeping his eyes firmly fixed on the inoffensive creature. He cowered his way to the far corner of the room and took refuge between two filing cabinets.

"For heaven's sake," I said. "Why are you afraid?"

"Me?" He laughed unconvincingly. "I'm not afraid."

"Terrified, then. It's only a chameleon."

"I don't like them," he said. "They're poisonous."

"Nonsense," I replied.

And to prove it, I put my little finger into the chameleon's open mouth and let it close its mildly serrated jaws on it. It did this several times.

"You see," I said. "No harmful effects."

"It's different for you," said the cashier, retreating even further between the filing cabinets. "You're a European."

"You mean they're poisonous to Africans but not to Europeans?"

"Yes, that's right."

I asked him whether chameleons had any other harmful effects.

"And another thing," he said. "Once a chameleon gets into your hair, you can never get it out."

"You don't really believe that, do you?"

"Yes, yes, it's true," he said, almost desperately. He was looking around for some route of escape, but I was at the door, and the window was barred.

"I'll prove to you it's not true," I said. "Just as I proved a chameleon is not poisonous."

I put the chameleon on my head where it perched like a pigeon atop a statue of a forgotten general. After a few moments in this ludicrous position, I removed it.

"There," I said. "Satisfied?"

But an African's hair was different, he said. A chameleon would never disentangle itself from an African's hair. I did not ask how one would get there in the first place.

I removed the chameleon from the office, where it had held up work for long enough. But the question of why so harmless a creature should inspire such terror continued to intrigue me. I asked each of the office workers, and the answers I was given were various but not quite frank. If a chameleon spat in your eye, you went blind; cuts inflicted by its tail never healed; the touch of its skin was corrosive. These answers were designed, I suppose, to deflect my clumsy questions. And everyone prefaced his remarks by saying they believe: they being their ignorant and superstitious countrymen but never themselves. Having cowered to a man, they denied ever having been afraid of my chameleon, now that it was safely at a distance. And I was told that peasants – but not, of course, accounts clerks – believed the chameleon was responsible for the black skins of Africans. God, when He put the Africans into the great oven to be fired, charged the Chameleon with the task of removing them when they were baked, but the Chameleon, slow and indecisive as ever, left them too long, and they were burnt.

I had not penetrated the inner thoughts of my workers, and

perhaps I never should, but of one thing I was certain: their fears were not of this world. And these fears were felt equally by the peasant and the doctor of philosophy; mere education did not expunge them. All one needed to seize power in Ngombia were a hundred or two chameleons, strategically placed.

The terrors of the villagers were never proportional to actuarial risk. They fled, panic-struck, from dangers that existed only in their minds, but cheerfully courted disaster that was all too easily foreseen. I suppose we had totally different conceptions of the world, or perhaps it was different worlds we inhabited.

There was a steep hill just beyond Mbaba, climbed by a road surfaced with scree upon which even the best of new tyres frequently slipped. In the rainy season the road ran with mud and was almost impossible to ascend. Every week our help was asked to remove the dead and injured from the site of an accident there.

But example never made the drivers cautious, quite the contrary. They drove with reckless abandon, as though challenging the hill to do its worst. One day Christopher and I drove together up the hill. A battered old green army truck had tried to climb it, but its engine had proved unequal to the task and its brakes too had failed, so that it started to slip backwards. Only a boulder at the edge of the road stopped it from plunging into a hollow below the road, but the shock of the impact on the boulder had pitched the passengers riding (illegally, of course) on the top of the truck into the hollow, followed by the sacks of maize on which they had been sitting. Seven of them died, suffocated by maize; one woman, too shocked to grieve, had lost four of her children, their dust-covered bodies now lined up neatly at the side of the road, as precisely graded in size as the pipes of an organ, waiting to be taken away.

In the bottom of the hollow two chickens, erstwhile passengers also, pecked among the sacks of maize and found one that had split, revealing to them untold plenty. The belongings of the passengers hung like forlorn flags of surrender from stunted bushes, their cardboard suitcases, formerly held together by string, having burst open. Down in the hollow, zombie-like, moved survivors, searching for their rags, while the army captain and the sergeant who had been driving when the accident happened complained bitterly. Unless the maize was moved to a safe place before nightfall, they said, there would be none left by the morning – the villagers would take it away during the night.

"You don't know these people, sir," said the captain, wheezing beery breath over me.

Christopher and I put some of the bodies into the back of my car, to transport them to Mbaba for burial. I had never seen or touched a corpse before: dead weight is no idle expression. As we drove away, the engine labouring in low gear, Christopher spoke.

"They say this place is full of bad spirits, sir," he said.

"Why do they say that, Christopher?" I asked, concentrating hard on the road ahead.

"So many crashing," he said. "So many crashing."

To the right and left were the rusting carcasses of crashed vehicles, stripped of anything that might have been useful.

"Does that surprise you?" I asked.

"People they say, why so many crashing here, sir?"

"Overloading," I said. "The terrible road, lack of maintenance, bald tyres, carelessness."

"But why people are careless, sir, here, only here?"

I saw the trap Christopher was attempting to lay. He wanted a chance to say it was the bad spirits that made people careless.

"They're drunk usually," I said.

"But why they are crashing here, sir, only here?"

This was untrue. All along Ngombian roads, at regular intervals, there were wrecks of trucks and cars that had gone off the road. For the purposes of our discussion, however, I overlooked this inaccuracy.

"Why is it, then," I asked, "that Europeans never crash here?"

"Our spirits cannot kill Europeans, sir."

"Well that's a comfort," I said, exasperated by his lack of reasoning, as I saw it. "Now I know I'm safe, I can drive carelessly."

It became important to me (I cannot say why) that I should be able to prove to Christopher the non-existence of spirits. It was belief in spirits that led to fatalism, I said, and it was fatalism that held Africa back. For a time, I was a missionary in the service of logic, or so I thought. But Christopher was stubborn and would not see the conclusiveness of my arguments. In a last, desperate effort to convert him to good sense, I offered to go with him to the village graveyard in the dead of night, but not unnaturally he refused to contemplate so bizarre a course of action. The spirits, he said, could smell the presence of a European – smell was the word he used –

and would remain safe in their graves, besides which, if the villagers learnt of his strange nocturnal expedition, they would assume he was plotting evil and kill him.

The village at night was an eerie place. We city dwellers have forgotten how dark darkness can be. It was so intense, this darkness, that it seemed not merely the absence of light, but to have positive, and not benign, qualities of its own. The glimmer of oil lamps in the village did nothing to lessen it, and as you drove along the road, your headlights cleaving the gloom as Moses cleaved the Red Sea, you encountered the maledictory glare of owls in the moment they took wing from the road. Even a confirmed materialist was glad to arrive home.

But if the spirits were everywhere, they did not affect the lives of everyone in the same way. While they could kill, they could also make prosper. In particular, they had assisted Faustin Kabarege to become the richest man in Mbaba. He owned the Disco Bar and the only privately-owned motor vehicle in the village, an old blue pickup truck. As monopolist, he could charge what he liked to transport the desperately ill to the nearest mission hospital, in Ongea. He also owned the only powered maize mill in Mbaba. He maintained his monopoly by sharing his profits with Mr Komba, who would have refused a licence to anyone else, in the unlikely event of an application.

Christopher said it was obvious the spirits favoured Faustin Kabarege because he had started out in life no better than anyone else. What other explanation could there be?

Yet there was another explanation, and it was Christopher who gave it me, at night in one of the village bars. I had decided that at least once I must sample the social life of the village, or what was the point of being in Africa? Christopher came, for he was one of the few Africans in Mbaba with whom I could enjoy more than a perfunctory, polite conversation. There was a hurricane lamp on our table – one of only three in the village – but there was no kerosene with which to light it. The mud-walled bar was stifling. The warmth inside was clammy and cloying, like that of a bed unaired for days. My appearance in the bar caused something of a sensation, for no-one from the plantation – no European that is – had ever come before, and I doubt if any ever came again. It was my only visit. After a flurry of effusive but faintly embarrassed greetings, Christopher and I were left alone.

I was offered maize beer to drink in a filthy plastic mug which had been scooped through a cauldron of seething white fluid. It was covered by a grey scum flecked with ash from the fire and insects that had drowned in it. The foam seemed to heave in the cauldron as though alive, a bubble occasionally breaking its surface. It gave off an odour like a tramp's breath. Try as I might, I could not bring myself to swallow it, and seeing my distaste, the bartender offered me *Revolution* beer, said to be the last in Mbaba. Brewed as it had been in Ndinji, I doubted it was any the more hygienic, but at least I could not see what I was drinking. It was lukewarm.

Christopher had promised one day to tell me the story of Faustin Kabarege's rise to eminence, and of the part the spirits played in it. But he had subsequently shied away from the subject, not because he was afraid or superstitious, he said, but because he thought it might bore me, as it was a long story. I hoped the maize beer would loosen his tongue, and eventually it did, though at first he still kept his voice low.

"Faustin Kabarege is having many ears," he said.

It seemed to me that the spirits had very little to do with Faustin Kabarege's ascent, unless it was they who caused the rains to fall that turned the road for months on end into an impassable river of mud. For it was the rainy season that provided Faustin Kabarege with his first opportunity. The potholes in the road were deceptively deep and if the wheels of a heavily-laden truck lodged in them, the truck was stuck until the rains eased and the potholes dried out. Since the road was wide enough only for one truck at a time, all other vehicles in both directions were held up too.

The drivers of the stranded vehicles had no choice but to live for a time in or under them until the weather improved. But constant vigilance was difficult to maintain, and one morning they would wake to discover that in the night their vehicles had been deprived quietly of two wheels or more. So even if the road now became passable, they were immobilised: they had to walk to Mbaba to seek help.

By a remarkable coincidence, Faustin Kabarege would have in stock the very wheels the driver needed to get started again. The price was high, of course, and if he could not pay in cash he paid in kind – from the back of the lorry. The driver knew better than to complain to the police, who had been squared in advance and who, far from investigating the loss, would only have added a fine for being in charge of an unroadworthy vehicle.

I said to Christopher that none of this appeared to require the intervention of the supernatural for its accomplishment, and he admitted that Faustin Kabarege and his men used often to give nature a helping hand by adding depth to the potholes or digging entirely new ones, to ensure a steady supply of helpless vehicles.

"He is using his brain," said Christopher without irony.

Another of Faustin Kabarege's enterprises, this time in conjunction with the bus drivers of the region, seemed to me also to require no assistance from the spirits. The driver of a bus laden with both passengers and their belongings would pretend the bus had broken down – plausibly enough, for in Ngombia buses continually broke down – and the passengers would alight to watch that no-one stole their baggage from the roof. Suddenly the bus would drive off, leaving the passengers in the road, while a few miles further on, at a prearranged place, the driver would deposit the belongings in the bush for later collection by Faustin Kabarege. The villagers of Mbaba were happy with this arrangement because they had a constant supply of clothes, at a price. They did not enquire too closely where they came from, for they all knew.

"But Christopher," I asked, "what has all this to do with spirits?"

The beer had by now made Christopher loquacious, and he became quite frank about my obtuseness. No man, he said, could venture out into the dark as frequently as Faustin Kabarege without the protection of the spirits. No-one would attempt it. And how was it that Faustin Kabarege always knew precisely where a truck had stuck?

"You said yourself, Christopher, that he and his men dug the holes..."

"Yes, he is using his brain, but how he know where to dig the holes? Who tell him?"

"But what has that..."

"And why the drivers always go into the holes?"

"It isn't easy to see them."

"And why no-one else is finding the baggage, Faustin Kabarege only?"

He pitied my scepticism. He told me another story: if this did not convince me, nothing would. It was the story of the *real* foundation of Faustin Kabarege's fortune.

One day a truck carrying a cargo of miscellaneous illicit goods crashed a few miles from Mbaba. The driver was injured, and the passengers fled into the bush to avoid the groans of the injured man, which were regarded as an ill-omen. Faustin Kabarege heard of the accident before anyone else in the village (how? asked Christopher pointedly) and went out to the stricken truck and driver. He was trapped in his cab, his leg crushed and broken. Was he glad or afraid to see Faustin? At any rate, Faustin knew at once what he must do, and he did it: he finished the driver off. He threw the body into the bush (why was it never found? asked Christopher) and took possession of the truck and its contents. With the proceeds, he bought his pickup, his bar and his mill, and there remained a plentiful supply of ready cash.

I asked whether the source of his wealth was generally known in the village. Not only in the village, said Christopher, but in the entire region: he was highly respected, for he had used his brain, and no party man ever passed through the village without calling on him. And what did the village people think of him? Well, there were some who were envious of his pickup and his mill, and of his good fortune in general, but naturally they were afraid to move against him because he was so powerful. But what of the murder, I asked, what did people think of that? It was a long time ago, said Christopher, eight or ten years, and people had almost forgotten it. It wasn't a good thing to have done, but *the man had used his brain*. These words seemed to excuse everything, and the spirits helped those who helped themselves. They approved of boldness.

I was confused, and not just by beer. What did Christopher believe? On the one hand he inhabited a world of unseen spirits, and on the other a world of ruthless self-seekers by comparison with whom New York brokers were as Franciscan monks. In any case, Christopher was now growing too voluble for his own good, for as he himself said, Faustin Kabarege the murderer had ears everywhere. I steered him outside. In the darkness of the village, he grew frightened by the indiscretion of his disclosures. Faustin Kabarege, to say nothing of the spirits, would now be his enemy; and he asked for the next day off so that he could take appropriate protective measures. This I granted him, and we parted, I to my suburb in the jungle, he to his dark hut haunted by dread.

A day later, having consulted a village oracle and done whatever was necessary, he appeared in the office more cheerful than ever. In fact, he was smug. Round his neck and wrist he wore a ring of dirty black cord – his protection from harm, he said. And he added that the best form of defence was attack.

After two months the spirits, ever inconstant in their interventions in the affairs of men, began to turn against Faustin Kabarege. It was announced over the radio that, to combat the black marketeers, economic saboteurs, speculators and spies who were impeding the attainment of full Human

Mutualism, the government, guided as ever by the party, had decided to exchange the present banknotes for those of a new design, in the process bringing Filosofa's portrait up to date, for it had to be admitted that he was no longer a young man. The exchange was to take place at the end of the week, short notice being essential to defeat the enemies of Mutualism. The banks were to change no more than ten thousand per person, the sum considered by Filosofa to be the most anyone could have accumulated honestly, or at least legally, in Ngombia. Of course, ten thousand was scarcely enough to buy even a pair of shoes on the black market (there was nowhere else to buy them), and at first, I assumed the people with an illegal stash of money would panic. But on the contrary, it was those with only a thousand or two who panicked.

In the first place they had to reach Ongea, where the nearest bank was. And the moment the exchange of banknotes was announced, the bus fare to Ongea quadrupled, so that much of the money was consumed by the fare alone. The line outside the bank was so long it took two days to reach the counter, and the town having been invaded by villagers from all around, the price of food rose dizzily. A swarm of bees attacked the line and stung one man to death. Those who fled had to buy back their places from those who hadn't or return to the very end of the line. And of course, the clerks at the counter expected *something for lunch*, as they called it, for exchanging the money. A peasant who left Mbaba with two thousand was lucky to return with five hundred.

For those with millions, however, it was different. *They* stood in no line. With their cases bulging with cash, they would walk straight into the manager's office and there – at a discount of perhaps ten per cent – have their money changed within five minutes. No records were kept, so there was nothing to fear. And as for ten per cent lost in the transaction, it would soon be made up by higher prices.

The announcement of the exchange therefore caused Faustin Kabarege no anxiety – at first. But it was necessary for him to recover his money from its hiding place, in biscuit tins buried in one of his fields. He had not trusted the bank, with its alarming propensity to lose all record of deposits; and he feared to keep the money in his house because of wives, burglars and impromptu searches by the People's Mutualist Militia.

Early in the morning, at the first light of day, Faustin Kabarege sneaked off to his field with a hoe and shovel. He had not marked the place, for fear someone else might dig there, but it was engraved upon his memory. When he dug, however, he found nothing. He was not yet alarmed: perhaps he had mistaken the place by a yard or two. But when he dug wider there were still no tins. Had someone been there before him? The ground, however, was undisturbed. For three days and nights he dug as he had never dug before, from dawn to dusk and beyond. Nothing. The deadline for exchanging the money passed, but perhaps something might still be salvaged. A week passed, however, and still he had not found his money. It was now lost beyond redemption.

Learning of his loss, the people of Mbaba, formerly so respectful of him, were beside themselves with glee. Filosofa was right to an extent: the Ngombians were egalitarian enough not to like rich men, though they wished to be rich themselves. Despite his loss, of course, Faustin Kabarege was still far richer than they: he had his pickup, his bar and his mill. But once the tide of affairs had turned against him, and the spirits had demonstrated they no longer favoured him, there was no escape from the downward spiral. It would not be long before the pickup was a wreck, the bar closed down and the mill defunct. They would not be replaced, yet whatever the inconvenience to them, the villagers would still gloat.

It was proved beyond doubt that the spirits had wished to destroy him when the tins of money were found in another of his fields.

"Who moved the tins, sir?" asked Christopher triumphantly. "No-one," I replied. "He just forgot where they were, that's all."

Faustin Kabarege's decline from then on was precipitous. Where once he had been energetic, he became listless. Where he had been fat and his skin had shone, he grew thin and his skin dried and cracked. Where he had been respected, he was now despised and laughed at. It was as everyone had predicted: his pickup broke down and was left to disintegrate; no-one supplied his bar any longer with maize beer or drank there, and it closed. For lack of a nut and a bolt, his mill ground to a halt. He no longer cared. He wandered aimlessly around the village, disorientated and increasingly shabby, barefoot when once he had worn only imported shoes. The transformation was swift and terrible.

When I left Mbaba, he was a prematurely old man in reduced circumstances. A few months earlier, he had been in the prime of life. His wives left him one by one, and he started to talk to himself. A month or two after I returned home, I had a letter from Christopher, addressing me as *Father*, to tell me that Faustin Kabarege was dead. He had wandered in front of a bus and been killed.

"And now Father," wrote Christopher, "are you believing in the Spirits of Mbaba?"

THESIS V

Human Mutualist democracy is not a matter of different parties, endlessly disagreeing. On the contrary, it has adopted our village tradition of consensus.

Filosofa Cicero B. Nyayaya

The baboons were very troublesome that year. So also were the wild pigs. They came from the surrounding bush to eat the maize as it ripened in the fields. Baboons by day, pigs by night: between them, they could destroy the labour of a season in a few hours.

Everyone in the village had a piece of land on which to grow his food. Christopher took me one day to see the plot that Mr Komba had allocated him. I had never before ventured beyond the broad main street of Mbaba, and I was surprised to discover how far the village extended. There was no overall plan, of course, just meandering paths of beaten red earth between widely-spaced huts. Some of the huts were decorated with zig-zag patterns of different coloured clays, others were devoid of ornamentation. There were no tin roofs beyond the main street, only roofs of thatch, and around each hut was an area of impacted ground where nothing grew, which snakes could not cross, and where harvested maize was spread on mats to dry in the sun, watched over by small children to shoo away the hungry chickens of the village. Each hut had a small, open storeroom where pitchers of water were kept. Banana trees with shaggy and untidy leaves shed a humid shade, while piebald goats, tethered to posts, tried without ever becoming discouraged to slip their leashes.

It was quiet, and everything looked rather attractive until you met a small girl of ten, clad only in a filthy piece of torn sacking, with a pitcher of water two thirds her height on her head, or carrying a heavy bundle of firewood, which it had taken her an hour or more to fetch. Life without the conveniences of the last century or two seemed suddenly less enviable. How, I wondered, did one light a fire without matches? Was it, perhaps, a tedious business?

Apart from the fetching and carrying, however, Mbaba was sunk in sloth. No-one did anything to improve his lot, to escape the grinding poverty. I explained to Christopher that *this* was the difference between Europeans and Africans. The men of the village, for example, idled their time away in the main street, chatting or showing off in front of one another, while the women sat on crude wooden stools in the shade cast by their huts – drunk, even at that early hour of the morning. Some of them were merely propped up against the mud walls, their withered breasts hanging like overripe fruit from a tree, while around them children with fly-covered sores crawled listlessly in the dust. It was as though a scene from some black rural Hogarth had come to life.

The air was sour with the smell of fermented bamboo juice,

ujanzi, which was tapped twice a day and fermented within twelve hours. The season for it lasted six months, six months during which a good proportion of the village was never sober. With so much to do to improve the village, I felt a surge of anger at this passivity, this idiocy. The expression on the faces of the women was as vacant as that of the tethered goats. Christopher and I, walking towards his land, crossed the village stream in a valley where the ground was wonderfully fertile but completely uncultivated. Anything would have grown there. The thought of the lost opportunity made my muscles tense with frustration. There was no reason, I said angrily, why five tomatoes in the village should cost a day's wages.

"Why don't people grow things here?" I continued. "Instead of sitting about doing nothing."

"They are razy," said Christopher, who always had difficulty distinguishing r's and l's. "But why?" I sputtered. "They are hungry, yet they grow nothing. Why?"

Christopher repeated his assertion, but admitted there was another reason too. He had once desired a plot of this fertile land to raise vegetables, but Mr Komba had refused him permission. Perhaps it was as well, said Christopher, since the other villagers would only have stolen his produce, partly because they wanted it, and partly because of envy.

"Why should they have been envious?" I asked. "You were only going to do what they could have done themselves."

"They are razy. It is more easier to steal."

And he told me that the villagers had held a meeting to decide what to do with this exceptionally well-favoured land. Under Mr Komba's expert ideological guidance, they had decided to do nothing with it, for fear of enriching some above the level of others, thus introducing un-Mutualist distinctions into the village. Besides, Mr Komba's powers of patronage depended on shortages...

We crossed the stream. The fields beyond were dry and irregular in shape, like pieces of a jigsaw, separated by lines of cassava bushes or vague paths that left plenty of scope for entertaining disputes over who could use what. It was more than thirty minutes to Christopher's land, and the sun's heat seemed to throb in pulses. If the people were lazy, I began to see why.

We reached his fields, no different from the others, where young green shoots of maize sprouted from laboriously heaped ridges of earth that ran in parallel but not straight lines through the fields. Christopher was proud of his land – his, of course, only until Mr Komba gave it to someone else. Because it had been at the outer edge of the village, Christopher had not only hoed it by hand but had cleared it of bush also. Because he was a young man and comparative newcomer to Mbaba, without influence of any kind, Mr Komba would probably allocate him next year a further couple of acres of bush to clear, while someone else altogether enjoyed the fruit of Christopher's present labours.

"But it's very unfair," I said. "They can't do that to you."

"Why not?" asked Christopher, laughing. "This is Ngombia, sir, this is Ngombia. Money speaking, only money speaking."

That Ngombia was Ngombia explained every injustice to Christopher.

"But why do all that work for nothing?" I asked.

"I have to eat, sir. Often you cannot buy food. It is too much expensive."

"Then why don't you try another village?"

"No job in other village, sir. And Mr Komba in every village."

We walked round his fields. Not being even a gardener, I was unable to offer advice. But I had heard that the yields in the village were only a fifth of those on the plantation.

"I hope you are weeding, Christopher," was all I could say. Christopher was offended.

"Weeding is woman works," he said.

And then it suddenly occurred to me that his fields were miles from any road. Filosofa's enlarged villages were all very well, as far as schools and clinics were concerned, but many of their fields were far from roads.

"How will you move your crop, Christopher" I asked.

He pitied my simplicity: he would carry it, of course. Thirty hundredweight sacks along the track I had found strenuous, unloaded as I was: I revised somewhat my opinion of the laziness of the villagers.

In the event, however, there was no transport problem because there was no crop to transport. Against the baboons Christopher had taken precautions, in the shape of a village boy whom he paid a few coins to sit all day and watch over the fields. His presence was sufficient to deter the baboons, apparently. I saw him there, staring blinklessly into the unmoving sky. Was his mind as motionless, or was he rapt in thought? There was no defence, though, against the night-raiding pigs, for nothing would induce a boy to venture into the fields in the dark.

It was the pigs that destroyed Christopher's fields. They charged out of the bush and trampled down the ripening maize, and then ate it with great efficiency, leaving nothing behind but leaves and broken stalks. In a few nights of porcine riot, Christopher's crop was decimated, and all his efforts set at naught.

Christopher was very upset, naturally. But what he wanted to know was why the pigs had picked *his* fields. I said it was because his fields were adjacent to the bush where the pigs lived; next year, he must ask Mr Komba for land well within the cultivated area of Mbaba. Impossible, he said, but I promised to help him with a bribe.

As things in the village transpired, the destruction of his crop was not entirely to his disadvantage: it saved him from accusations of witchcraft.

That year the pigs and baboons were more numerous than anyone could remember, and they destroyed most of Mbaba's harvest. The baboons evaded drunken sentries (*they are using their brain*, said Christopher of the baboons), and the pigs completed the damage. But not quite everyone's fields were ruined, and this, in the end, caused a lot of trouble.

The situation was so serious that Mr Komba called a meeting of the entire village. Usually, the villagers came only reluctantly to such meetings and had to be threatened with collective fines; but in this case, the matter was so close to the villagers' hearts that they needed no second invitations. As the air cooled and the shadows lengthened, the villagers gathered at the football pitch next to the church and waited for their leader to appear who, as a matter of principle, was late. To keep the villagers waiting, Mr Komba once confided to me (after a few beers), had two advantages: it gave the impression he was a man so weighed down with duties that it was impossible for him to be punctual, and it made the villagers even gladder to see him when he came.

As always, the meeting commenced with a speech by Mr Komba. He had called the village together, he said, because there was a crisis facing it. The party, of course, could not sit idly by while the crisis worsened, for the party's sole interest, indeed its reason for existence, was the welfare of the people from whom it sprang. In the true spirit of Filosofa's call to self-reliance, therefore, and in the living spirit of Ngombian Human Mutualism, he had called the village together to solve a problem, a problem soluble only by the conscientious application of Filosofa's ideas. In short, the baboons had eaten all the maize, and what were they going to do about it?

Someone at the rear of the crowd, a notorious drunkard, suggested they should ask the baboons to give it back. There was a lot of laughter, but Mr Komba did not smile. He was taking his responsibilities as father of the village seriously, and I think he enjoyed playing the role for once of disinterested parent. He said it was all very well laughing now, but next year many of them would be short of food and they wouldn't be laughing then. On the contrary, they would be asking the party for help. Something had to be done.

Dominicus, the village idiot who spent most of his days walking at great speed up and down the road while wearing motorcycle goggles and steering an imaginary wheel in front of him, suggested that a big fence be built round the whole village to keep the pigs and baboons out. Though no-one for a moment took his suggestion seriously, everyone began to discuss it at once, with great vehemence. Where would the poles for the fence come from? Who would pay for them? How high would the fence have to be to keep the baboons out? Would it keep them out at all, since they were so good at climbing? How quickly could it be built? This year or next? And what would happen when the village decided to increase the area under cultivation? These matters were debated passionately, as passionately as if anything depended on the answers.

The schoolteacher, to demonstrate his superior knowledge of the outside world, mentioned that in some countries, Australia for example, they used electrified fences, though he added he wasn't quite sure whether this was to keep the baboons out or the goats in. And then Thomas Mwingira, who had once been a mechanic for a year in Ndinji, pointed out it would be difficult to electrify wood, as anyone could see during a thunderstorm. And then someone else rose to remark that, lightning apart, there wasn't any electricity in Mbaba, not even any kerosene, and this in his opinion was a very serious problem, even a disgrace.

Amidst general applause, Mr Komba rose to answer an unjustified slur on his leadership. The party, he said, was doing its best, in fact it worked day and night, to ensure a continuous supply of kerosene to Mbaba, but – as Filosofa had said in a speech in Zurich only the month before – the world economic system was such that countries like Ngombia always suffered shortages. Until there was world justice, then, there would always be kerosene shortages in Mbaba. And Mr Komba added that anyone who said different was an enemy of the people.

Mr Komba's remarks, which were not fully understood by the villagers and therefore thought to be clever, subdued the meeting somewhat. But the mention of Switzerland touched off a brief invasion scare. The schoolteacher said that in *his* opinion Ngombia should crush the imperialist invaders, and that extreme vigilance was needed above all in the present situation.

The meeting by now had shown a marked tendency to stray from its original subject, a tendency reinforced by the arrival of two oil-drums of maize beer. All manner of matters were discussed, including the prospects of the Mbaba football team in its forthcoming match against a neighbouring village. There was general agreement that it all depended on who was the referee.

Eventually, however, the villagers did return to the subject of the baboons and their depredations. Someone reminded them that even as they discussed other things, wild pigs might be feasting off the remaining fields. He was asked angrily how he knew, to which he replied that he didn't know, but it was a possibility. A woman, very drunk, said that it was too late to do anything in any case: the animals had eaten everything.

It was then remarked that the baboons had not eaten everything: some people's fields had remained unscathed. And what one excited villager wanted to know was *why* they had remained unscathed. Having sown the seeds of discord, he sat down.

It was dusk now, a fire had been lit, and it threw flickering shadows. People had become drunk, and their thoughts turned naturally to witchcraft.

For it was clear that if some people's fields had escaped

destruction, witchcraft was involved. A motive was not difficult to find: in a year of dearth, those with maize remaining were at a double advantage. And it was well known that magic could influence the movement of wild animals. Hunters had always used magic, and they continued to catch animals, didn't they? So what was more obvious than that someone had used magic to call in the pigs and baboons to destroy their neighbours' crops?

An excited, if incoherent, discussion of magic in Mbaba followed, and it was agreed there was far too much of it about. These days people resorted to it for the most trivial purpose, not like in the old days when it was reserved for important things only, like killing an enemy. An elderly man – or so he looked, though one could never tell with the villagers – cited the example of his daughter who was growing very thin, had fevers at night that drenched her in sweat, and had lately started to cough blood. She had been ill for a year now, in fact ever since she refused to marry a young man from a nearby hut. If ever there was a case of sorcery, this was it, and all for a foolish love affair.

I was behind the trunk of a large mango tree so as not to be too conspicuous. Christopher was beside me, translating when I was lost. Hearing the old man's story, I wanted to shout, 'Your daughter has T.B., you fool', but I was unsure how my interference would be received. And the accused, very drunk and swaying as though onboard ship in a storm, began loudly to abuse his accuser. Surprisingly, he admitted the charge; he had laid the daughter low with powerful magic, he said, because she had insulted his manhood – he, one of the most successful hunters in the village or even the province. Unless the old man were careful, he too would find a powerful spell cast upon him.

Naturally, this confession inflamed the meeting further; and a few days later the young man was found in a ditch, badly beaten. He had admitted by then that his confession had been a vain, drunken boast, but it was too late to retract. His original confession, moreover, provoked a whole rash of accusations, from which it emerged that not a child had died, a seedling failed, a roof leaked, a pot broken, or a mishap occurred, but that a neighbour was suspected of witchcraft. The pigs and baboons were by now all but forgotten, and it looked as though violence might break out. It was Mr Komba who, in the end, saved the day. But his prefatory remarks were not well-received.

"Brother and sister villagers," he shouted above the general hubbub. "As you know, the Party of the Mutualist Revolution does not recognise witchcraft. In fact, it abolished belief in witchcraft by law twenty years ago. Under the constitution, witchcraft does not exist."

These remarks exerted a far from calming effect on the meeting, and everyone began to shout irrefutable examples of witchcraft.

"But... but..." shouted Mr Komba, holding his hand up to secure a hearing. "The party also recognises that nothing is more important than the People's will. I propose, therefore, that we deal with this matter in accordance with the principles of Human Mutualist democracy..."

"How? How?"

"I suggest we take a vote to decide who are the *real* witches in the village."

The problem was that almost everyone in the village had been accused, so Mr Komba suggested further that the eight people with the most votes be declared the true witches of Mbaba. Each villager was allowed to nominate one witch, and Mr Komba counted the show of hands. He kept the scores with a stubby pencil on a scrap of paper he found in the pocket of his greatcoat.

No-one escaped nomination. Husbands even accused wives if, say, they had borne no more than four children. In the darkness, in the still night air, with dancing shadows cast by the fire, the atmosphere of suspicion was inescapable. Yet I thought that the villagers, in a strange way, were rather enjoying themselves.

Mr Komba announced the results as though for an election to parliament, those with the fewest votes being mentioned first. Whether he used the opportunity to settle old scores I cannot say, and everyone was too drunk to tell. But as soon as the 'victors' were declared, they were turned upon with a vengeance born of relief. The denials of the elected witches were not believed; and it was said that, as was well-known, those wrongly accused of witchcraft were immune to the effect of flames. Let them, therefore, prove their innocence, if they so desired, by plunging their arms for ten minutes into the fire.

There was widespread support for this idea, but Mr Komba did not approve of it. Things were getting out of hand, and he regretted ever having called the meeting. Now that the witches had been identified, something would have to be done about them to satisfy the villagers, but Mr Komba wished to avoid anything that might reach the ears of his superiors and ruin his career. Filosofa, who was himself not above secretly consulting the entrails of a chicken to decide a question, had publicly denounced all forms of magic, witchcraft, divination and so forth, making them punishable offences. Unless he were prudent, Mr Komba faced disaster.

He therefore called upon the villagers to find a solution more in keeping with the ideals of Human Mutualism than ordeal by fire. Other ordeals were suggested, not less severe, but eventually someone mentioned a sorceress in a distant village famed not only for her powers but for the benevolent ends to which she put them. Surely, she had cunning enough to deprive the witches of Mbaba of their malignity?

Mr Komba grasped eagerly at this solution. Though a few villagers were disappointed at so tame an outcome to the drama, it was agreed that next morning the eight witches should be expelled, tethered together, in the direction of the sorceress's village, and that they should not return until they displayed visible sign of having lost their gift of magic.

I thought that the matter might be forgotten by the morning, dismissed as the inflamed suspiciousness of inebriation, but I was mistaken. No-one had forgotten the previous night's proceedings, and everyone except the eight witches was eager to put into effect the meeting's resolution. In the presence of the whole village, they were tied together by a rope and led out of Mbaba in the direction of the sorceress's village. They were warned not to try any tricks or to return before they had been exorcised, and they departed to the sound of jeering. One of the villagers even threw an egg at them, a measure of his strength of feeling, considering the scarcity of eggs. Meanwhile, Mr Komba remained in the background, dissociating himself from the expulsion.

Things might have been worse for the witches. True, they were condemned to walk for three days through the bush, and they would arrive at the sorceress's village tired and hungry; moreover, a stray lion had been seen along that path only a couple of years before. But no serious harm came to them. Ten days later they returned, minus the rope which they had sold en route at a profit, with their heads and bodies completely shorn of hair, their scalps beaded with sweat. With their hair had gone their witchly powers, and they were welcomed back to Mbaba without further recrimination.

While they were away, the baboons had eaten what remained of Mbaba's fields. A crisis loomed, but I detected no anxiety on the faces of the villagers.

THESIS VI

The principles of Human Mutualism are identical with those of the great religions.

Filosofa Cicero B. Nyayaya

The church, naturally, set its face against such remnants of paganism as magic, and did whatever it could to counteract them. But sometimes it was itself compelled to resort to magic, or the threat of it. I am thinking of that memorable Sunday in Mbaba when the collection plate went missing. How it was stolen without anyone in the congregation noticing is a mystery, for the plate was large and awkward in shape, not easily secreted even under the most voluminous overcoat. But disappear it did, and when it became clear that it was not going to be returned, a voluble discussion broke out as to where it might have gone and what had happened to it. Someone suggested its disappearance was a miracle, but this was rejected on the ground that the village was full of thieves, besides which miracles were good events, like the recovery of a pig after it had been knocked down in the road, not bad ones like the disappearance of the collection plate.

Our priest, a small young man newly ordained, was very angry. The church was one of the few organisations in Ngombia that depended on market forces: the priest needed the proceeds of the weekly collection to live. If he allowed the crime to go unpunished so soon after his arrival in Mbaba – he had been with us only a month – he would lose the scant respect to which his small stature, his youth and his supposed celibacy entitled him. It became for him a matter of imperative necessity to recover the plate.

Unhappily, this proved by no means easy. It was not possible to lock the doors of the House of God with the congregation inside, for the purposes of a search. Besides, the thief had probably slipped away. The priest suggested that perhaps someone might have taken the plate by accident, not realising what he was doing, in which case could he please return it? But this charitable interpretation of events only provoked laughter and a further fall in the priest's stock. Appeals to the better nature of the thief, promises of forgiveness, reminders that there was more rejoicing in heaven etc., produced no impression except that of weakness. It was not only the money but the plate itself that would be difficult to replace. The young priest had no choice but to appeal to the bishop.

The bishop of our diocese was a large man who, when not officiating in church, wore a safari suit of many colours. He also wore a clerical collar and shirt of scarlet or purple, and around his neck hung a huge crucifix, a foot long and six inches wide, attached to a chain strong enough to leash a fair-sized dog. On his forefinger he wore a large ring like a knuckleduster: it had to be big, he said, because people were forever genuflecting and kissing it, and he didn't want them to miss and kiss his fingers instead, which was unhygienic.

He had the face of a potentate, highly mobile in a jowly kind of way. He was balding on the crown of his head, and the back of his neck was wrinkled into thick folds. He was generally affable, even hail-fellow-well-met, but by all accounts given to outbursts of furious rage at the slightest provocation. He appeared to have only two moods: loud joviality and insensate anger. If you wanted to flatter him, especially if you were a white man, you had only to call him *my lord*. Then you were his friend, if not for life, then at least until the next time he saw you, when he would greet you with a powerful slap on the back that would propel you quite a few yards.

I first encountered this man of God in his 'palace' in Ongea, where I had gone on business. I was asked by our priest to deliver his letter about the missing collection plate to the bishop. The palace did not really deserve the name, except perhaps by comparison with a mud hut. It was a large building, two storeys high and built round three sides of a square. All the windows were louvred and this in itself was a testimony to the bishop's power and influence: for replacing a single louvre in Ngombia was a task that required diplomatic and rhetorical skills (as well as money). The palace was furnished with ugly, solid upholstered furniture and decorated with cheap European bric-a-brac such as musical gondoliers with a ballerina on the prow, and brass models of vintage cars, arranged on shelves so that the eye could not avoid them. On the walls were the extravagantly emotional pictures of popular religion, as well as those of Parisian *gamins* with impossibly large, tearful blue eyes. And in pride of place in the bishop's best room, with an elaborate frilly lace cover, was a video set, another sign of the bishop's great power and influence.

But for all its furnishings, the palace remained a strangely empty place, a mere shell of a house, more a temporary encampment than a permanent home, upon which even the bishop's large personality had not been able to stamp a character.

As I was shown into the palace, I heard the yells of a small child coming from the direction of the verandah. I went out to investigate and found the bishop with a boy of about six under his arm, to whom he was administering a sound beating. When the bishop saw me, he set the child upon his feet, told him to go away, and helped him to start in that direction with a firm smack. Then the bishop turned to me.

We shook hands and I noticed he was panting as a result of his recent exertions. As some men feel an irresistible urge to laugh at funerals, so I am impelled to say something sarcastic to men of the cloth.

"Spare the rod, spoil the child," I said.

"The little rascal came on to the verandah while I was drinking tea," said the bishop. "He wore no shoes, and his face was dirty."

He signalled me to sit down in the cane chair and sat down heavily himself. The tea things were on the table.

"Care for some tea?" he asked. "That would be nice," I said.

"Martha! Martha!" He called for his servant to come and grew irritable when she failed to materialise at once. "Martha! Martha!"

Eventually a plump woman who moved as though through

treacle emerged from inside to pour us two cups of tea. It would have been much easier to do it ourselves, but the bishop had his standards to maintain. He sat back in his chair.

"I didn't become bishop to be treated with such lack of respect," he said, referring now to the small boy. "He ought to be dressed properly when he comes to see me. That is why I beat him. For the sake of the Church."

"A wise son maketh a glad father," I said.

It was, perhaps, an unfortunate choice of proverb.

"He is not my son," said the bishop explosively. "He is my nephew. He lives with me because his parents are... his parents are dead."

I smoothed his ruffled feathers by calling him *my lord* a couple of times, and before long he was happily, even ecstatically, telling me about himself. In many ways he was a remarkable man, and he knew it. He had been born in a mud hut, the sixth child of an ordinary peasant, and had gone to a missionary school where his exceptional academic ability was soon recognised. He was marked out for a career in the church and attended a seminary. From there he was sent to Europe for higher theological studies, completing his thesis (in Latin) on the perfections of God in St Anselm's ontological argument. He was one of the first African bishops in Ngombia and no doubt carried a cardinal's hat in his knapsack.

One could not but admire his unlikely accomplishments, yet I felt they were external accretions, like barnacles, rather than part of his very fibre.

He read the letter from Mbaba and at once began to fulminate against the impiety of the peasantry, whose disrespect knew no bounds. But he would soon bring them to their senses. He rose from his seat and paced up and down the verandah in agitation. Yes, he said, he would soon show them – a stiff-necked people – the power of the church, which would not tolerate their heathen ways. The bishop knew the peasants better than they knew themselves – had he not been born one of them? Yes, he said, he would come up to Mbaba next Sunday. It was a threat as much as a promise.

He kept his word. He stormed into the pulpit next Sunday magnificently attired, his mitre nodding furiously, his crook banging on the floor from time to time for emphasis. And he harangued the people of Mbaba as they had never been harangued before. They were risking the Wrath of God, he said, they were a stiff-necked people, like the Hebrews, except they were not chosen, far from it. Therefore, unless the collection plate and its money were returned within two weeks, he – the bishop – would cast a spell over the thief and all his family, accomplices and friends. Let them rest assured that when he cast a spell, it stayed cast. (Two weeks' grace was a masterly touch, I thought, for the bishop knew the money would already have been spent and the plate sold, and hence it would take time to recover them.) The church, he continued, would be left open at night so that the thief could return the plate without revealing himself to the village; a notable instance of mercy, the bishop said, more than the thief deserved, but if he tried to short-change the church in any way by so much as a fraction of money, the spell would still be cast.

With that, the bishop descended from the pulpit and swept out of the church.

His threat was not strictly in accordance with orthodox theology, perhaps, but it was effective. On the tenth day after its utterance the plate mysteriously reappeared in the church and the doors thereafter were locked at night as usual. Our priest held a service of thanksgiving.

Shortly afterwards, the village turned to the bishop for help in quite another matter. Mbaba was unhealthy, even by Ngombia's standards: it was notorious for its malaria and other fevers. But the village clinic was always short of supplies, even of the simplest drugs, and the staff demanded high payments for administering whatever little there was. To be admitted as a patient to the clinic, its floors and walls caked with old blood and other mementos of previous patients, was regarded in the village as a virtual sentence of death. Nothing was ever washed for lack of soap and willpower, the food prepared in the primitive kitchen went to feed the staff rather than the patients. At night the clinic was in complete darkness, and anyone wishing for attention had to scream, first to wake the attendant and then to guide her steps through the blackness of the night. Staff and patients shared their hopelessness.

The villagers were stoical in the face of suffering and death, but experience had taught them, despite their superstitions, that medicine could sometimes help them. Looking around, they saw that some villages were provided by the church with clinics, and that these were always better staffed and supplied than government clinics. Why, they asked, should Mbaba not have a church clinic, especially as its need was so great? They asked the bishop for help.

He was not a man, I should imagine, much given to Good Works for their own sake; on the other hand, he enjoyed displaying his extensive foreign connections to the awe-struck gaze of his fellow-countrymen. And it so happened he had just received a letter from a group of charitable ladies in England asking whether they knew of any worthy cause, preferably of a medical nature, for which they could raise money. He asked the villagers to give him a few months at the end of which they would certainly have their clinic, and he wrote to the charitable ladies, painting a picture of medical desolation that would have moved hearts far less susceptible than theirs.

The villagers were pleased that they had obtained a new clinic on their own initiative (self- reliance, Mr Komba called it), the bishop was pleased to have demonstrated the extent of his influence, and the charitable ladies (I surmise) were delighted to have found a worthwhile object for their activities. Only the staff in the government clinic were unhappy, for with church competition the price of aspirin in Mbaba would fall.

The burden of illness became for a time more supportable by the villagers, buoyed up by the prospect of a new clinic. The bishop sent them progress reports, relayed from Europe. The ladies were proceeding well, baking cakes for sale at charity bazaars, secure in the knowledge that each mouthful represented ten babies snatched from the jaws of million-murdering death. How glad they were that there was such suffering in the world to relieve!

But then, imperceptibly, hope began to slip away from the villagers. Although the bishop continued to report that all was well, that funds were accumulating fast, and that work on the clinic building would soon begin, somehow it never did begin. Soon, any day now, said the bishop, and the villagers even went so far as to clear a piece of land for their new clinic. But as the months went by and a whole year passed, hope changed to disappointment, disappointment to apathy. The cleared land reverted to scrub, and the new clinic was all but forgotten. There was relief among the staff of the government clinic.

Then, suddenly, the bishop revived hopes and raised them higher than ever before. He sent a message to Mbaba to tell them he was arriving in person to make an important announcement. It was assumed he was coming to inaugurate the building work (for which the villagers intended to charge the church handsomely). But the bishop was only visiting Mbaba en route for Ndinji, to attend a conference on the Theology of Development. Nevertheless, the villagers went to some trouble to welcome him, putting on dances and even slaughtering a goat.

The bishop did not stay long – it was a tiring journey to Ndinji. Practically everyone in the village turned out on the football field to greet him and hear him speak. He looked serious and stroked his crucifix once or twice. He had something to tell the villagers, he said, something which they might find rather disappointing, but he had every confidence that they would take it as the good Christians and Human Mutualists they undoubtedly were.

His friends in England, he continued, who had so generously collected money for Mbaba's new clinic, had discovered a more urgent need elsewhere. Africa, unhappily, was full of good causes, some of them even better than Mbaba's new clinic. The bishop urged the villagers to consider: their land was fertile, there was plenty of it, the rains had not failed in living memory, it was easy for everyone to grow enough food. Unfortunately, there were many parts of

Africa where this was not so, where their fellow-Africans suffered not only from lack of land, but drought and the death of their goats as well. The bishop looked grave. He was sure the villagers would understand, and even applaud, the decision of the English ladies to give their money where it was more urgently needed.

There was a slight murmur of discontent, and the bishop left rather abruptly. It had not escaped notice that he arrived in a brand-new Range Rover with tinted windows and stereophonic cassette player. The sound of music emerged powerfully from the splendid vehicle as he drove away. It was, I think, the only time a Bach cantata was ever heard in Mbaba.

Thesis VII

Ngombians have always believed in the goodness of Man.
That is why Human Mutualism is possible in Ngombia.

Filosofa Cicero B. Nyayaya

If you stood in the centre of Mbaba, you saw hills in the
distance richly green except at the extremes of day, when they
seemed to have been washed blue and mauve by
watercolourists. Halfway up one of the hills nestled a brick
church, built by German missionaries more than half a
century before in the Bavarian style, so that the little metal-
covered onion dome at the top of the tower flashed and glinted
in the sun. The German missionaries were gone, replaced by
a few Spanish nuns and a remarkable Spanish father.

The mission was reached along a treacherous dirt road that
twisted and turned (for no obvious reason) and had stretches
where sharp rocks protruded through the mud or dust. Two
swampy streams were crossed by means of old pontoon
bridges that had been known to collapse. Most of the way was
through virgin bush in which there were said to be lions. I
never saw anything larger than ground hornbills, however,

with black plumage and enormous red bills, that hopped clumsily away as one passed, and which looked like notaries in operas.

I first met Father Ordoñez as I took a walk along that road one Sunday morning. I had not intended to reach the mission, which was ten miles away; I was only taking a casual stroll. It was hot and humid, the kind of day that makes you feel unwashed the moment you emerge from the shade, and I rather regretted having started out at all. I was thinking of turning back when a Land Rover, far from new, rattled to a halt beside me and the door was flung open for me to get in.

The driver was a European in his late forties; he was slightly overweight, had raven black hair and the kind of beard that never looks freshly shaved. He was wearing rather old-fashioned clothes, none too clean, that told you at once he was a man uninterested in appearances. He had intense, dark brown eyes that fixed you like a beetle to a board.

We introduced ourselves, and he asked whether I should like to come to lunch at the mission. I thought it might prove interesting and agreed at once. We drove off.

A few hundred yards further up the road an old couple, bent by age, flagged us down. Each of them carried a gnarled stick for support, and they spoke with the tremulous voices of the aged. They were on their way to the mission village, and they climbed laboriously into the back seat, which had been designed with the robust rather than the infirm in mind. They had difficulty too with the mechanism of the door handle, so that it took them in all several minutes to establish themselves in their places. I noticed with surprise that Father Ordoñez passed these minutes impatiently: for I should have expected the old couple to arouse only compassion.

I was again surprised when, instead of starting off at once, the couple and Father Ordoñez began a conversation, too fast for me to follow. It rapidly became heated, at least on his side. The old couple said less and less and became apologetic and cringeing. At the conclusion of the conversation, they climbed out of the Land Rover as laboriously as they had climbed in, and only then did Father Ordoñez start up the engine. I watched the old couple in the mirror disappear into the dust-clouded distance. "What happened?" I asked Father Ordoñez when they were out of sight.

"They wanted a lift to the mission," he replied tersely.

"Then why did they get out?"

"I told them to. They didn't have their fare."

My face must have revealed my surprise, for Father Ordoñez continued without further questions.

"They knew my rule. I don't take anybody unless they pay a small contribution to the cost of the journey. I made this rule ten years ago. These people must learn that everything costs money, and money costs effort."

"Everything costs money?" I said. "Not the most important things, surely?"

"Every material thing," he said. "They are too used to being given things for nothing. They think the white man is here just to give them everything they want. This aid has given them the wrong idea. It has spoiled them."

Although Father Ordoñez stared intensely through the windscreen with his piercing eyes, he still managed to hit every rock in the road.

"And yet," I said, "for all the aid they receive, these people are still very poor. They wear rags. They have nothing."

"They have nothing because they do nothing. They want things but do not want to work for them. That is bad faith, it is like stealing. I have to teach them another way."

"But that couple was so old," I said. "Surely it would have done no harm..."

"Old or young, they are all the same: something for nothing. They must learn. And if I give one a free lift, then I must give all a free lift."

"But what about the Sermon on the Mount?" I asked.

"You can forget the Sermon on the Mount," said Father Ordoñez. "You're in Africa now." He accelerated over a particularly large boulder, and I thought the Land Rover was going to shiver into a thousand pieces. There was something terrifying about this man, about his consistency; but he was fascinating too. He had been born in the wrong century: he should have been one of those priests who went to America with the conquistadors to supervise the forced conversions. I am not a phrenologist, but I should say that Father Ordoñez's bump of doubt was not well-developed.

We reached the mission village, which was more primitive than Mbaba: that is to say, there were no tin roofs. The mission itself was a collection of pleasant buildings of small red brickwork, constructed round cloister-like courtyards. Trees grew in the courtyards and spread their shade. As for the church, it was simple but graceful. The interior was without decoration, except for a mural above the altar. It depicted Christ, painted in the days when he was undoubtedly a white man, gently indicating heaven with his right hand and hell with his left. The latter had been more vivid in the artist's imagination. Heaven was but a cool hillside town with white stucco buildings, deserted but for a few men of indeterminate race, all of them dressed in white linen suits and panama hats, wandering like holidaymakers in search of the eternal *table d'hôte*. Hell, on the other hand, was much more definite: green-scaled saurian devils with pitchforks herded scores of black men and women into a dark pit. Crimson flames, stoked by black furry demons with long tails, awaited the sinners at the bottom. And under this minatory tableau was an epigraph in Ngijwi concerning the straightness of the gate and the narrowness of the path etc.

I couldn't resist asking Father Ordoñez whether to him also hell was more vivid than heaven. He replied that they were equally real, for each required the existence of the other, hell being the conscious deprivation of heaven and heaven being the full understanding of hell while not dwelling there. It was all very abstruse and bleak.

We walked from the church to his living quarters. His room was cell-like and, though cluttered, absolutely spartan. His bed, his table, his chair and his cupboard were as simple as design could make them, avoiding ornamentation as though it were heresy. His curtains were unpatterned, of a rough and drab-coloured cloth, and there were no pictures on the walls, only a crucifix, more as an aid to devotion than decoration. Scores of books were piled on the floor, occupying every corner. There was nothing frivolous, amusing or even merely literary among them, only works of Thomist theology and philosophy, and textbooks of tropical agriculture and development economics. Did his intellect never tire, I wondered? Did he never long for mere diversion?

The room in which we had lunch was, by the standards of Father Ordoñez's cell, almost comfortable. Next to the dining table was a coffee table and four maroon upholstered armchairs. Shelves nearby contained not only works of piety and papal biography, but copies of old Spanish newspapers as well.

The meal was prepared by one of the four Spanish sisters at the mission, but neither she nor any of the others ate with us. The meal was served by a half-wit village boy, taken into the mission for the sake of charity. There was little contact, I learnt later, between the sisters and Father Ordoñez. They never ate together, not even on Christmas day. The sisters ran a small clinic, but on quite different principles from those of Father Ordoñez. They were kindly, straightforward creatures (straightforward, that is, except for whatever had driven them to embrace their lives of self-denial), and their goodness was of the instinctive and unreflecting kind. They accepted patients from wherever they came, charged them nothing if they said they could not afford the small fees, and in general thoroughly undermined – in Father Ordoñez's opinion – his efforts to teach the people the virtues of forethought, honesty, thrift, scrupulosity and self-reliance. And Father Ordoñez was not the kind of man who could accept fundamental disagreement about matters of importance to him without the embitterment of personal relations. His conception of right and wrong was too clear-cut to admit of any compromise.

Lunch was served in a chipped enamel casserole. It was a kind of paella, mainly glutinous rice, with occasional peas, grains of maize and fragments of grey meat buried deep within it. It had very little taste.

"You are fortunate to have come to lunch today, Sunday," said Father Ordoñez.

Ungrateful by nature, my thoughts did not echo Father Ordoñez's words. I sipped at some sickly, tawny-coloured altar wine, so sweet that one felt sticky all over after only a mouthful.

Father Ordoñez explained that it was only on Sundays that he ate anything resembling European food. The rest of the week he ate the maize porridge of the Africans, as a gesture of his identification with their poverty. It was only when he had returned on leave to Spain and had been discovered by doctors there to be suffering from malnutrition, that his superior in the order had directed he should henceforth eat European food at least once a week. Even then, Father Ordoñez took pride in sabotaging the superior's order by issuing himself only a tiny portion of meat and vegetables; and he viewed even this poor paella as an indulgence of the flesh pardonable only because of his vows of obedience.

I asked him whether he thought the Africans understood his gesture of solidarity.

"Of course not," he replied. "They think I am mad."

I began to wonder myself. He had been making the gesture now for more than ten years, and still they had not grasped its meaning. Was it not time to give up? It was the belief of the villagers that white men could have anything they wanted; for a white man, therefore, to live in poverty, to eat the villagers' miserable and unvarying diet, was perverse to say the least. And so a rumour began to spread, I heard later, that Father Ordoñez, under cover of missionary zeal, was in reality panning for gold in the nearby river, for it was agreed that no man could *choose* poverty when the alternative was limitless wealth. For a couple of nights, the villagers even posted watchmen to catch Father Ordoñez on his way to the river, and when he failed to materialise, they attributed it to his superior cunning rather than error in the rumour. What man would immure himself in their village without ulterior motive?

The meal over, we sat at the coffee table, and Father Ordoñez poured us each a glass of Spanish brandy, carefully suppressing any indication of pleasure (if indeed he felt any). He sipped the brandy as though it were medicinal only. There was an awkward silence while I cast around for something to say.

"I see you still take the Spanish papers," I said at length, relieved to have found a subject.

"Yes," he replied. "But I do not read them. Spain is not the country it was."

I took him to mean that Spain had changed, and not for the better, since the death of the *Caudillo*.

"But now you have freedom in Spain," I said.

"Freedom!" he exclaimed, as though spitting out something distasteful. "Spain was free enough before. It was the freest country in the world. You could go anywhere in perfect safety. And now? What do they want with their so-called freedom: Freedom to read and write filth, freedom to write what they like in the newspapers regardless of the truth, freedom to commit crime without punishment, freedom to murder unborn babies and to break marriage vows, freedom to rape young girls and old women, freedom for atheism and immorality... no, there is no discipline anymore, no truth. Spain has been destroyed by this freedom of yours."

There seemed no possibility of taking this discussion further, and it was Father Ordoñez himself who proposed a walk, despite (or perhaps because of) an old back injury that gave him pain when he walked.

We started out towards a hill that overlooked the mission and had a small shrine dedicated to the Virgin Mary at its brow. To reach it we had to walk through some of the village. Father Ordoñez had a word for everybody, even those slumped drunkenly against the walls of their huts. They replied, but with none of that warm and almost indiscriminate friendliness I had come to expect of them. Machiavelli's words ran through my mind: it is better for a prince to be feared than loved.

We clambered up the hill, he suffering from backache, I from breathlessness. But he would not stop on the way – he made no concessions to agony. At the shrine the statue of the Virgin was very eroded, hardly more than a small white pillar now, with the facial features erased by the wind and rain, though her hands, embracing the world, had 'miraculously' been preserved. Nearby was a smooth, sloping boulder, convenient for lying on. Here we recovered our breath and surveyed the village below. One could tell at a glance which were the villagers' fields and which the mission's. The latter were symmetrical and orderly, the former haphazard, giving the impression they had barely been scratched from the earth. Beyond the village we could see the land stretching a hundred miles, and it was this, perhaps, that gave our conversation its abstract, even metaphysical turn.

Eventually we came to discuss what could be done for Africa, a continent where, in the midst of potential plenty, the people lived a life that – according to Father Ordoñez – was indistinguishable from that of beasts (except for drunkenness). Africans were very close to nature, he said; a hundred years ago they were naked and would be so again if the foreigners were to leave.

"They are very primitive," he said. "They cannot think logically. They live only for the day. They have not developed a sense of morality."

"And yet they are happy," I said.

"They are happy as a pig at a trough is happy."

"But why try to change them, especially when you cannot guarantee them anything better?"

"Is knowledge better than ignorance? Is health better than disease? Is the Sistine Chapel more beautiful than a mud hut?"

When Father Ordoñez was roused he could be eloquent: but his eloquence was that of a hard, contemptuous certainty. It occurred to me that if ever he turned his talents to evil ends, he would be a dangerous man.

"You don't seem to like or respect these people very much," I remarked.

"It is not a question of whether I like or dislike them. This is where God needs me."

"How do you know?"

"I have prayed."

It was the first time I had heard Father Ordoñez speak of God, and it was almost as of an equal. Father Ordoñez needed God, but God also needed Father Ordoñez. And the God in whom he believed was the vengeful, irascible, fickle and sentimental God of the Old Testament.

"It must be difficult," I said, running my eyes over the

village and the mission, "to teach the message of the Gospels to people who have no morality and live only for the day."

"Difficult?" he said. "Impossible, rather. It is as natural for these people to steal, lie and cheat as for them to breathe. If you tell them to love their enemy, to forgive those who have wronged them rather than to take revenge, they think you are mad and laugh at you. I do not try to teach the Gospel. They are not ready."

"But..."

Father Ordoñez interrupted my protest. He told me I did not know Africa, I had been there only a few months, I could afford to keep my sentimental illusions because I was not going to stay, but he – he was going to spend the rest of his life in this place and so had better understand the people as they really were.

"You talk of teaching them forgiveness," he said, going somewhat beyond what I had said. "Let me tell you a story of how Africans understand forgiveness..."

The mission, he said, ran a small seminary for about twenty youths. He knew most of the seminarians had no vocation, they came to the seminary only to receive the secondary education that would qualify them for a government job in Ndinji. Even those who wished to remain in the church were aiming at the bishop's palace rather than the vows of poverty. They cared nothing for the disciplines of religious life, though they liked the music well enough. They stole and cheated and lied just like any other Africans, but Father Ordoñez (secretly) prided himself on the sharpness and shrewdness of his eye, which kept their misdemeanours within bounds.

Well, during a religious holiday last year the seminarians

had been attending an early morning service when a villager rushed in to tell them that a neighbour of his was taking advantage of the absence of the religious community to harvest for himself some of the maize in the mission's fields. At once the seminarians abandoned the service and ran to the fields, where they caught the thief *in flagrante delicto*. They dragged him back to the mission, gave him a sound beating, and locked him in a cupboard while they looked for transport to take him before the magistrate in Mbaba.

There, of course, the thief denied his crime – until, that is, the policeman who was acting as prosecutor in the case jogged his memory with a few well-aimed blows on his head, already tenderised by the seminarians' drubbing. The latter watched with undisguised delight. This changed rapidly to disappointment when the sentence – eighteen months' hard labour – was passed. The magistrate explained that under the law, a man who stole less than a hundred kilos of maize could be given only such a sentence. Now, if he had stolen more than a hundred kilos, it would have been different...

If they had known the law, said the seminarians, they would have let the thief continue stealing until he had gathered more than a hundred kilos, as was obviously his intention. It was therefore unjust, they said, that he should be given the lighter sentence. And then they crowded round the magistrate who, rightly or wrongly began to feel threatened, so he added three years to the thief's sentence to placate them. The seminarians returned to the mission happy and fulfilled.

"And these are the Africans," added Father Ordoñez, "who know the Sermon on the Mount by heart."

The conclusion I was intended to draw was clear enough.

A silence fell between us. "But if you don't teach the Gospel," I said after a long pause, "why...?"

"Why am I here?" Father Ordoñez anticipated. "This is where God intends me to be. And just because I do not teach the Gospel does not mean I teach nothing."

"Such as?" I asked.

"These people," said Father Ordoñez, sweeping his arm round the village, "are like children. They are children, intellectually and morally. They have the understanding of children, perhaps less. And when you teach children, do you start with the most difficult lessons? Do you teach them Shakespeare before they can read, geometry before they can count?"

"No, of course not..."

"No. Well then, in the same way I cannot start with the Gospel in all its sublimity. I just lay the foundations. I must teach them other things first."

"What other things?"

"First, I teach them personal responsibility. I teach them that each man has his destiny in his own hands."

"And has he?"

Father Ordoñez judged that my question was frivolous and ignored it.

"These people think that everything they want can fall from heaven. They do not see that how they live is the result of what they do. They think everything is magic or fate."

"And you want to change all that?"

"It has been changed already." Father Ordoñez was exultant – I could tell by his eyes. "I have changed it. After ten years, during which I prayed for the strength to continue, the villagers have begun to understand at last. Oh, many times have I doubted whether my way was the right way, but now I have been vindicated. How do you say in English – you have to be cruel to be kind?"

"What has happened? What has changed?" I asked.

"Ever since I came here," said Father Ordoñez, "I have grown maize in the mission fields. I am not a farmer, you understand, but in Spain I grew up in a village surrounded by farms. I read how to grow maize, and every year I grew five times as much as the villagers."

He concealed his pride well; he mentioned it only as a matter of indisputable fact.

"At first," he resumed, "the villagers thought it was magic. It was the only explanation they could think of. Time after time I told them they could grow as much maize as I if only they followed the same method. But they said, 'No, that is how you Europeans do it – we Africans do it differently'. And every year, they came to the mission for food when theirs ran out. Of course, I made them pay for it. I wanted them to realise my maize had not just fallen from the sky. It had cost effort. But still they wouldn't follow my methods."

Father Ordoñez stared into the distance. I asked him what had happened then. The fine muscles of his face flickered as he struggled to conquer an expression of triumph.

"This year they came to me to ask me to teach them how to grow maize."

This seemed scant reward for ten years' residence in the back of beyond, but then I was an accountant, not a missionary. Father Ordoñez explained that this was the first step in his larger plan to save the villagers' souls. Once they understood, through their agricultural efforts, the concept of personal responsibility, then – and only then – would they understand the choices demanded of them by Jesus Christ.

It sounded rather far-fetched to me, and I said that if the villagers increased their output, it would be more for the sake of Sony Walkmen than for their eternal souls. But Father Ordoñez replied that he was not so foolish as to forget the importance of material incentives. As a reward for the villagers' request for help, he was purchasing two oxen for the village, which would reduce considerably the onerous burden of tilling by hand. The oxen would demonstrate to the villagers that if they made the right choices, God would reward them.

"But *you* are providing the oxen, not God," I said.

"I am guided by God. I am his instrument."

Father Ordoñez stared once more into the distance – at infinity, I should think. It would have been difficult at that moment to question the identity of God's will and Father Ordoñez's actions.

The oxen, said Father Ordoñez, would revolutionise life in the village. It was all very well for foreigners – here he looked at me – to criticise Ngombians for their laziness, but had any of them tried to till two acres with only a hand hoe? It was gruelling, back-breaking work; but now, with oxen to help them, the villagers would be able to plough more and with less effort. They would be free at last to do other things.

"Like drink?" I asked.

"Some, perhaps, but not all. They will do handicrafts, grow vegetables."

Father Ordoñez explained that they drank so much only

because of the hopelessness and stagnation of their lives. I repeated that they seemed happy enough to me, but he said this was only a superficial impression. He knew them better.

We left our vantage point and returned to the mission. The descent was more painful for Father Ordoñez than the ascent, for it was hard to stop oneself from running, and each step jarred his back like an electric shock. When we reached the mission we had some tea, dark and bitter, and then Father Ordoñez drove me back to Mbaba. On the way, I asked him whether he believed in Charity; and he replied, in certain circumstances. This was a deep and serious question, not a matter for idle speculation, by which he meant, of course, that I was not a fit person with whom to discuss it. I knew from his cell that he was a man of intellectual interests, who more than likely considered each decision he made, even on unimportant matters, from first principles. But his was the kind of intellect that flourished in isolation, without dialogue except with itself, without criticism, without the play of opposing ideas. He was an intellectual hermit and did not wish me to break into his solitude.

The oxen arrived in the village, so I heard, and Father Ordoñez began to train them, taking some of the villagers with him so that they should know in future how to train oxen. When the animals were broken in, he presented them to the villagers, with the injunction that the benefits should be shared among them equitably.

The advantages of oxen, Father Ordoñez had explained to me, were that they had no running costs in foreign exchange, seldom broke down, needed no spare parts, held their value and provided fertiliser – unlike tractors.

Some weeks later, I visited Father Ordoñez again. Sundays – particularly the afternoons – hung heavy, and though I cannot say I altogether liked Father Ordoñez, I found him interesting and even rather admired him. Living in a small community as I was, I craved a change of face and conversation. Such a change came to seem of transcendent importance.

Father Ordoñez greeted me neither warmly nor coldly, but almost as though he had been expecting me. He was one of those men whom nothing surprised, at least outwardly, lest doubt be cast on the power of his intellect. He asked me in for coffee. We sat round the coffee table, and I leafed through an old magazine. Small talk was not among Father Ordoñez's accomplishments, and it was up to me to think of something to say. I was curious about the oxen and asked how the villagers had taken to them.

To my surprise, I received no answer at all. Whether Father Ordoñez heard my question I cannot say. Instead, he began to talk of general economic and social conditions in Ngombia, and he asked me whether I should be interested to read an essay on the current situation written by a missionary priest who had once been a professor of political science in a Canadian university. The essay was full of diagrams, with words like ASPIRATION and IMPLEMENTATION enclosed in boxes with arrows, running in both directions, between them. Oxen were not mentioned in the essay.

Later, though not through Father Ordoñez, I heard the story of the oxen. A few days after he had entrusted them to the care of the villagers, Father Ordoñez took a walk through the village. By all accounts he was feeling pleased with himself for having effected a greater change in the life of the village than any that had occurred in the last fifty or a hundred years. Though usually a man of the utmost self-control, he could not forbear to nod graciously to everyone he met. Before long, however, he was aware that something was wrong: it was more like a Sunday in the village than a weekday, with people slumped against the walls of their huts in drunken contentment. But there was more than mere drunkenness about them, a kind of greasy repletion after a feast. Soon Father Ordoñez discovered the truth. The villagers had slaughtered the oxen and eaten meat until they were intoxicated with it, until they staggered with the weight of it in their stomachs and collapsed, stuporose, in or near their huts. There being no means in the village to store the meat, they had had to eat the slaughtered oxen within two days, and this they had done.

So not only had Father Ordoñez's plan to revolutionise the agriculture of the village failed, but it had had precisely the reverse effect. For at the busiest time in the agricultural year, it took the villagers a week to shake off the lethargy induced by the feast, and that week was lost to the fields. God proposes, Man disposes.

A lesser figure than Father Ordoñez might have been crushed by this setback, but so secure was his knowledge that his was the only way for the village that, apart from a certain reticence in discussing oxen, he was soon restored to full vigour. But the villagers resented – so I was told – his insistence that they pay for any little services the mission rendered them. They believed that Father Ordoñez was enriching himself at their expense. They preferred the sisters who, out of natural generosity, believed any hard-luck story they were told and gave away whatever they had. Father Ordoñez, however, was not courting popularity; nor was he concerned, I think, to do good, at least in the commonly accepted sense. No, his purpose was firmer, harder than that: he was the sole interpreter of God's word in the village. Father Ordoñez lived modestly, but he was not a modest man.

A consequence of his coldness and aloofness was that his occasional acts of charity and compassion were inexplicable and puzzling to the villagers. The sisters were difficult enough for them to understand: why should anyone abandon a life of plenty to minister to complete strangers, not even relatives, who were moreover poverty-stricken? But at least the sisters clearly *liked* the villagers, and their kindness therefore transcended incomprehension. But Father Ordoñez had nothing but contempt for the villagers, they knew that; why else should he exhort them continually to change everything in their lives, from the way they grew maize to how they disposed of their excrement?

And so when Father Ordoñez gave shelter in the mission to two albino girls who had been all but outcast as accursed by the villagers, there was much speculation as to his motives. The girls were hideous to behold, so much so that it took an effort of will to look at them steadily. Their hair and eyebrows were orange-yellow, their eyes a raw pink, and they darted back and forth as though everything scorched them. Their skin was also pink, dry and cracked; they looked as if they had been rubbed down with sandpaper by a furious nurse. Disfiguring their skin further were heaped-up, strawberry-red sores upon which flies fed contentedly. These girls could not stand long in the sun and so were useless for work in the fields; and having been rejected from birth by everyone, they had no personality, but were like wild animals in their timidity. Yet Father Ordoñez took them in and gave them rooms near the seminary.

The shade of the mission buildings was grateful on the albinos' delicate skin. They had no occasion to leave their new home. Father Ordoñez treated them with no particular favour, but neither did he evince disgust, which was kindness enough. He expected them to perform small chores around the mission in return for their keep and to remain unobtrusive when visitors called, but this they were glad enough to do in any case.

Then one day, several months later, Father Ordoñez was seen leaving the mission in the Land Rover with one of the girls. It was said her stomach had swollen greatly of late, and Father Ordoñez was taking her to another mission with a large hospital.

Father Ordoñez expelled one of the seminarians, but the villagers were not fooled. At last, they understood this stranger in their midst; or thought they did.

Thesis VIII

Health care for all is a basic principle of Human Mutualism.

Filosofa Cicero B. Nyayaya

In the town of Ongea was a large government hospital. It was not highly regarded by the people, and anyone who could afford it went to the nearby mission hospital. A Bulgarian surgeon (no-one knew what unforgiveable crime he had committed to be posted there) did not improve its reputation. And the rumour that one of the doctors in the hospital forcibly abducted children from the street to drain them of their blood, which he then sold to patients desperately in need of it, caused the children of Ongea – and not only the children – always to run past the hospital, if they could find no route, however circuitous, to avoid it altogether.

The hospital was a collection of long pavilions, connected by covered walkways. There had once been gardens, but now there was only dust with tufts of spiky grass. Everywhere were strewn the remains of ambulances, here a door, there an axle. On the larger panels of the defunct vehicles were the words *The Gift of...* or *Presented by...* The hospital, it seemed, had been the object of many charitable donations, but still there was no ambulance to transport the injured or dying from even a hundred yards away, though one could usually be found to take the cousin of the director's third wife to the far end of the country.

Dogs roamed in packs between the wards. You always knew when a woman had been delivered of a baby because the most ferocious barking would break out behind the maternity ward. The discarded placentas would be thrown into the dust where the dogs fought over them. The strongest of the dogs were very well-fed indeed.

The patients – those who could still walk – sat outside the wards in the dust, their heads, arms or legs wrapped in bandages through which the blood had seeped and congealed into black tar. It was widely said that if you entered Ongea Hospital with one disease, you left – if you left at all – with two, and I knew of a child who entered the hospital with burns and was discharged with typhoid. The nurses walked slowly between the wards, scuffing the ground with their bare feet, animated only when they met one another for a chat. Their uniforms were white, with all manner of stains, buttons missing and holes; their white caps with frilly edges perched at every angle on their hair, not rakishly, but from inertia.

The hospital was known officially as the *Bishop Herbalgoode Memorial Hospital*: there was a notice, somewhat faded, to this effect at what would have been the gate had it not been removed long ago. And in the director's office, next to the picture of Filosofa and looking down on a desk piled high with dusty, yellowing files, was a bleached picture of a handsome young English priest – Father Herbalgoode as he then was –

who had early espoused the cause of Human Mutualism and was a friend of Filosofa's, some even said a decisive influence on him, and his spiritual guide. No-one knew any longer whether Bishop Herbalgoode had ever had a special connection with the hospital, or whether it was named after him because all of Filosofa's friends had institutions named after them. In any case, the local people did not call it the Bishop Herbalgoode Memorial Hospital: they called it *Numba a Faazi*, the House of Death.

The hospital was not without its uses, however, as one day the villagers of Mbaba discovered: for it was only at the hospital that a death certificate was obtainable. And while in the general way whole generations could live and die without interference from birth and death certificates, just once in the history of Mbaba a death certificate assumed a decisive significance and contributed to the welfare of the village, as the villagers saw it.

During the rainy season it was not uncommon for the number of babies that died of malaria and various intestinal diseases greatly to increase. The mosquitoes found places to breed, and all the filth of the village seeped into the water supply. But that year the number of deaths was excessive, even for the rainy season, and almost every day there was more than one procession of mourners, serious at the front, chatting and joking at the rear, to the burial ground, preceded by the mother with a tiny bundle wrapped in cloth. Naturally, such a development did not go unremarked, and very soon people were discussing why in this, of all years, so many babies should have died. There was no general meeting about it, but consensus was reached nonetheless. Not surprisingly, it was witchcraft that had caused the babies to die.

There was only one candidate for the role of evil genius. He was an old man living on his own in a hut on the edge of the village. He had a son who worked in Ndinji and sent him money from time to time. The old man was otherwise without relations and unusually – for the villagers were sociable people – he sought no-one's company but was content to pass out his days tending a tiny plot and sitting in his hut. At the best of times, his eccentric behaviour excited unfavourable comment, but these were not the best of times, and no-one stopped to ask himself what motive he could have had for wishing the babies' deaths, what benefit he derived from them. His aloofness alone was sufficient to condemn him.

It was rumoured that he had a collection of herbs in his hut, a not unlikely circumstance since almost everyone in the village over the age of thirty fancied himself something of a herbalist. But in the inflamed temper of those times, which many villagers enjoyed, it was regarded as a suspicious circumstance, if true; and three young villagers with a taste for drama, not often satisfied by life in Mbaba, volunteered to establish once and for all whether the old man had collected magical herbs with which to depopulate the whole village (for it was by now generally agreed that he was trying to kill everyone). One afternoon, then, with the old man dozing in his hut, the three young men crept inside and found it was just as everyone had suspected: there were small mounds of herbs everywhere, and even dried lizard tails. Of course, they would have found the same things in half the huts of Mbaba, but that did not give the young men pause: they woke the old man and gave him a stern warning. Either he desisted from his magic or it would be the worse for him. The old man appeared bemused by what they said, but they were not fooled. The three young men insisted he knew what they were speaking of.

But still the babies died. They grew thin, their eyes seemed to fill their whole face, their skin wrinkled and then they were so listless it was difficult to say exactly when they died. There was clearly a malevolent spirit about, called into action by magic, and something would have to be done if Mbaba were to survive.

The three young men met in the evening and drank maize beer until they were brave. Then they went to the old man's hut and dragged him from his bed (a cardboard box flattened on impacted mud). Out in his plot, they beat him. Whether they meant to kill him, or only to give him a warning, will never be known. Probably they beat him with no clear idea in mind and were content to let God decide between life and death. But he was a frail old man and he died.

His body was found next day. No-one in the village mourned him: they simply buried him in a shallow grave in the bush, having performed a magical ceremony to devitalise his angry and evilly-disposed spirit. And strangely enough, after his death the number of babies that died *did* decrease. The drier weather had set in, and the epidemic was over, but the villagers were utterly convinced that it was the old man's death that had brought the improvement about.

Naturally, in a village the size of Mbaba it was impossible to conceal for very long the identity of the murderers. Even if they had not boasted of the deed, certain as they were of having performed a valuable public service, the villagers would soon have known who they were. And the three young men were right – at least to begin with – in thinking they were perfectly safe from retribution, for they were regarded not as criminals or dangerous killers, but as heroes who had saved Mbaba from a terrible evil. The police, who must have known everything, did nothing, for they agreed with the rest of the villagers.

Thus, everything would have been settled to everyone's satisfaction had not the old man's son suddenly decided to visit his father in Mbaba. This was about a month after he was killed. The son was a minor bureaucrat in Ndinji, the importance of whose position the old man, in his infrequent conversations with the villagers, had liked to exaggerate. The son was therefore respected, feared, admired and disliked. When he arrived in Mbaba, everyone told him his father had died of natural causes: a combination of malaria, cancer, pneumonia, old age, a stroke, his heart and dysentery. Why, he asked, had he not been informed of his father's death? We didn't know your address, the villagers replied. Then why did you not send a message over Radio Ngombia, as was frequently done in such cases, asked the son. Forgive us, but we are only stupid villagers, they replied. The son did not believe them, the more so as they were unable or unwilling to show him his father's grave. And before long he had heard the whole story from the village idiot, the one who wore motorcycle goggles and walked up and down the road with an imaginary wheel between his hands.

Armed with this information, the son questioned the other villagers more closely. Eventually, in anger, they admitted his father had been killed, but it was only what he had deserved. After all, he had been trying to kill the whole village. As for the three who had done it, they ought to be rewarded rather than punished.

The son went to the police. His father had been murdered, he said, and furthermore the identity of the killers was known to everyone in Mbaba. He demanded that the police at once arrest the killers, but the police denied all knowledge of the case, even that his father had ever existed, then claimed he had died of natural causes; and finally that the whole affair was nothing to do with them. For if there was no body, how could there have been a murder?

The son was far from satisfied. It was no longer merely a question of filial duty but of bureaucratic satisfaction. He wanted to show these villagers that you didn't trifle with a man from Ndinji. I found him one morning hitching a lift by the roadside down to Ongea, where he knew the deputy commissioner of police. I picked him up. On the way he poured out his indignation to me: not about his father's death, but about the way he had been so disrespectfully treated by the police.

"Don't they know who I am?" he said. "But I'll teach them one lesson."

I left him in combative mood. He saw his friend the deputy commissioner and then returned to Ndinji, satisfied that he had defeated the villagers. And sure enough a police Land Rover entered Mbaba a few days later, full of policemen with machine guns. Whether they had bullets was not known, but it was certain they arrested the three killers and took them roughly away. The villagers were angry at this injustice, but they knew their anger never swayed the authorities, quite the contrary. Some other tactic would be required to obtain the release of the village heroes.

A delegation was formed and a subscription raised. Before the delegation left for Ongea, however, ceremonies were performed by several well-known witchdoctors to ensure that if the delegates absconded with the money they would suffer from the most exquisite torments. This was necessary even though the delegates were close relatives of the three imprisoned men: for they had never had so much money in their hands before.

They went to the Bishop Herbalgoode Memorial Hospital. At first, they were refused admission to the director's office, but a small payment secured it. With the ceiling fan rotating creakily above them, they explained to the director what they wanted. The director made a few objections: not on principle, but simply to raise the price of his favour. He had never seen the old man, either dead or alive. How, then, could he sign a death certificate to say that he had died of natural causes? The delegates improved their offer, and after a brief tussle the director – a short man who was always polite, except with his staff – gave them the certificate.

They took it triumphantly to Ongea gaol, where the three men were languishing. There they were told to come back next day, as the governor of the gaol was 'not on seat'. Twice more they were told the same thing, until they were quite ready to pay.

They asked also to see their three imprisoned fellow-villagers. They had been in gaol only a comparatively short time, but they had already lost much weight. The prison rations were small for those without means to increase them, and the maize flour from which the porridge – the only item in the diet – was made was always infested with sour-tasting weevils. The men shared a small cell with seventeen other prisoners, one of whom was a lunatic and another an elderly Indian trader, arrested for economic sabotage because his small store had sold soap at seven times the controlled price.

That he had bought the soap at five times the controlled price, and his captors subsequently sold his stock at nine times the controlled price, was not taken into consideration, and though no guiltier than anyone else in Ngombia, everyone – even the other prisoners in his cell – rejoiced at his downfall. The lice, the food, the bucket of nightsoil, were all a peculiar torment to him, with his pride of race, but his very misery was a source of consolation to the others in the cell.

The prison governor was a man whose fatness had a strangely solid quality. The size of his waist was a matter of pride to him: he had worked his way up from nothing. He had the joviality of the despot: he shook when he laughed, and so did everything else. It was well-known he hired out his prisoners as labourers to whoever would pay and pocketed the money himself. He once offered the services of his prisoners to our plantation in Mbaba, complete – he said – with supervisors. We did not have to worry, he continued, that the prisoners were criminals, murderers and the like; for the guards were armed and had permission to shoot on sight. No-one would ask any questions. We rejected his kind offer, and I saw at once that we had made an enemy.

The delegates from Mbaba put the death certificate before him. It was proof, they said, that the three men were being unjustly held responsible for the death of a man who died of pneumonia, as the certificate stated quite clearly. The governor affected anger: he slapped the certificate down on his desk, demanded to know if he was a clerk that he should be asked to deal with certificate matters, and insisted irritably that they should have gone first to his subordinate who would have prepared a report for him. The truth of it was that the governor was very nearly illiterate, and the written word in any form reminded him of his weakness. He called in a clerk on the pretext of asking him whether the piece of paper was genuine or a forgery.

"You can't be too careful with these villagers," he said. "They're peasants."

He prevaricated. He said the law could not be subverted for anything or anybody: it must progress with its impersonal majesty. He hitched up his trousers. But he knew all the same the significance of the death certificate. Eventually, the men would have to be released, and *he* might as well be the one to benefit from it. As the Ngijwi saying has it, when a man's mouth is open, he doesn't spit out food. And so once more it was a question of agreeing terms. The governor did not want to sell himself too cheap, but he did want to sell himself. A compromise was reached as to the sum to be paid, more delicate negotiations followed about the actual mode of release, since the delegates did not trust the governor to release the prisoners once the money had been paid, and the governor did not trust the delegates to pay the money once the prisoners had been released. In the end, it was agreed that half the money should be paid on deposit, the rest cash on delivery.

But in the event, only two of the three men were delivered safely. The third, who as it happened had taken the lead in the affair and was a labourer on the plantation, began some days previously to behave rather oddly. He would shout out loud some piece of nonsense and then strike a peculiar pose and remain adamantly silent. Of course, odd behaviour was by no means unusual in the gaol, and at first no-one took much notice of him. Then his ranting grew more insistent, and sweat ran down his face in rivulets. Finally, he fell on to the ground, his eyes glassy and staring, and he could not get up. He had cerebral malaria.

On the day the others were freed, then, he was carried to the *Numba a Faazi*, the House of Death. He was put in a dark ward where the shutters were kept firmly closed against noxious fresh air, while the air inside was stagnant with suppurative odours. In the corner stood the cupboard of medicines, its doors torn off, its shelves stained red and purple from lotions spilt long ago and encrusted with dirt. The supplies were few: empty vials and old needles were strewn among the unwashed bandages. The ill man was all but thrown on to an iron bedstead without a mattress, but he was by then past caring for his comfort: he was unconscious. His relative – one of the delegates – stayed with him to pay the nurse to give him the injections he required. The relative, fortunately, knew the hospital well. He insisted on watching the nurse draw up each injection, for she would otherwise have substituted water for the drug, which she then would have sold outside the hospital. He even got her to wipe the needle on her dress before she used it for the tenth time that day. Slowly the young man began to recover from the malaria that had laid him low.

When he woke, he looked around uncomprehendingly. It was the first time his eyes had been open in three days. He did not know where he was: the ward was dark and shadowy. His relative tried to explain to him, but he was still confused and frightened. How had he come there? He could remember nothing of the days before his admission. Then suddenly he remembered his radio, his radio in Mbaba that was the envy of all his neighbours, of everyone in the village even, a radio that could speak foreign languages and play disco music so loud that the ground vibrated. It was his prize possession, almost his only one, something which marked him out from everybody else in Mbaba. It had been given him by a relative who had been abroad. Where was it now? He sat up, terrified by the thought that his radio might have been stolen, for where could he get another? A man might work for ten years in Ngombia and not earn enough for such a radio. His radio, yes, he must go and look for it. He tried to get out of bed.

His relative calmed him. The radio, he said, was safe in Mbaba, but he had been very ill with malaria and so it was essential he took rest to recover fully. The young man sat back exhausted, still muttering about his radio, not apparently reassured. He muttered on for an hour or two, then seemed to sleep. His relative crept away from the ward, to escape the boredom of his vigil and to search for food. While he was away, the patient woke and looked around him. Nothing was familiar. He started once more to rave about his radio and searched for it under his bed and under the beds of the other patients. The ward nurse sat drowsing at her table, her head resting on her folded arms. The patients who were awake found the young man's antics highly amusing. Discovering no trace of the radio in the ward, he wandered outside. The brilliant sun, which he had not seen for days, so blinded him that he staggered a little. He walked unsteadily through the grounds, still muttering about his radio, sometimes shouting. The patients, nurses, relatives and idlers who were always found in little groups around the hospital thought he was a madman who had escaped from ward ten, the ward for lunatics. They did not try to stop him as he went beyond the grounds of the hospital and into the street. Neither did anyone there stop him: they were used to escapees from the *Numba a Waloko*, the House of the Bewitched, who were either funny or dangerous, and in either case to be left alone.

Ongea was not a large town. Within fifteen minutes you could walk into the bush: bush that was as wild as any in the country. There were lions there, though not as many as formerly, when they imposed a kind of curfew on the villages in the area. There were other animals, though, and most of the little meat to be had in Ongea market came from the forest.

The young man wandered into the bush in search of his radio. A hundred yards from the road, the forest looks the same in all directions. A man in full possession of his faculties is lost there in a few minutes, unless he is an accomplished tracker. And as he searched for his radio, the young man went deeper into the forest.

He was found a week later by a party of hunters. He had died of thirst, with his radio on his lips.

When the villagers of Mbaba heard of his death, they knew the son of the murdered old man had employed a powerful witch in Ndinji. And if ever the son dared show himself again in Mbaba, they would know what to do with him.

THESIS IX

We have created a New Kind of Man – the Human Mutualist.
Filosofa Cicero B. Nyayaya

Athena, my housegirl, was in her late twenties. She had a round face with animated eyes, though it was many months before she would allow them easily to meet mine without lowering them or taking refuge shyly behind a door or wall. She changed the pattern in which her hair was combed almost every day: sometimes it was braided in lines, sometimes it was done into little tufts like antennae that made me think of Martians. She was very fond of finery though unable, of course, to afford much of it. I collected a few cosmetics or cast-off clothes from the plantation wives, and then Athena would appear heavily made-up in a silk dress, struggling to keep her balance on high-heeled shoes.

She walked to work every morning from the village, three quarters of an hour away. Her wages seemed to me very low, but she made no protest, and I was warned to pay only the going rate, or I should ruin things for everyone else, besides which, it was well-known that housegirls only wasted their money. I supplemented Athena's wages with gifts of soap, oil and rice, which she would not have been able to buy in Mbaba whatever her wages.

Athena was very poor and prey to every possible misfortune. She lived with her four children on a plot of land at the extreme edge of the village; with no money and no influential connections she had no hope of a more desirable plot. Her home was a mud hut of the simplest construction, with cracks in the walls through which daylight showed. On the inside of the walls she had stuck brightly-coloured advertisements from my magazines, messages from a life so alien I do not think she even dreamed of it. Her every possession, almost, was some unconsidered trifle I had thrown aside without thought, which she would diffidently ask to be allowed to take home with her. When I visited her there, the only chair she possessed was placed ceremoniously in the small dusty yard in front of the hut, and one by one the children touched my head with their outstretched palm and uttered the respectful words of welcome, *shika na goma*, I am under your feet. Spread on the yard was a mat on which the ripened maize sat drying, one of the children standing guard over it all day to prevent the marauding chickens from gorging themselves on it. Another child slowly ground the maize with pestle and mortar, while yet another fetched water. Usually, they had sores on their thin legs, wrapped in dirty rags, nourishment for the flies. In the rainy season the hut was all but hidden by the tall green maize scattered with sunflowers, sewn despite warnings from the Ministry of Public Health that such an arrangement promoted the spread of malaria.

Athena was not married, even in the village sense, and all

of her children were the offspring of different fathers. The first of them, born when Athena herself was little more than a girl, was called *Rahati*, which meant Good Fortune. Her fourth child, a boy, was called *Latatizo*, which meant Problem.

Unfortunately, Athena did not learn quickly from experience. Twice she fell pregnant in the eighteen months I knew her. She did not tell me, but asked for a loan, which she used to pay a wise woman in the village; and twice she needed a further loan to go to the mission hospital to be treated for the complications arising from the wise woman's treatment. I asked her to consider less hazardous methods of limiting the size of her family, but she never quite came round to using them.

I don't wish to give the impression that Athena was promiscuous, if by that is meant anything derogatory. It was simply that she was alone, without a father for her children, and very vulnerable. Twice her hut was broken into while she was away at work and all her possessions stolen. She needed a protector, and so she was – well, *hospitable*. One does not blame a man dying of thirst for not avoiding the temptation of a poisoned well. And there were plenty of men in the village, to say nothing of visitors and passers-by, to take advantage of her situation.

In other respects, too, Athena maximised her misfortune. She seemed unable to envisage the future, let alone provide for it. She was foolish with money, at least from my lofty standpoint. She did not use it to improve the diet of her children or herself, the first call – I should have supposed – on her income. No, she frittered it on attractive trifles. An itinerant photographer came once to Mbaba, taking instant pictures; he did such a roaring trade, despite the prevailing poverty (or was it because of it?) that the villagers actually fought to have their pictures taken first. Athena, mesmerised by the magic of the apparatus, managed somehow to struggle to the front of the mob with her children, and insisted on individual portraits as well as a family picture. The six photographs cost her an entire month's wages, but as the children began to appear on the magical squares of shiny paper, she thought the bargain a perfect one. It was one of the happiest moments of her life. It came as a bitter surprise later in the month to discover she had nothing left for food, and furthermore that the pictures were fading fast to an unrecognisable blur. Regarding me as the man who could do almost anything, she asked me to reverse this process; and when I told her there was nothing I could do, she said that if she had known the pictures would fade, she never would have spent her money on them. But even with this knowledge, I suspect, she would have been unable to resist their fascination.

She came to me not long afterwards for a loan to buy fertiliser. She had heard that a consignment had reached Mbaba. I was astonished that she had thought ahead to the harvest, and though I knew the money would never be repaid, I lent it her. I asked the price of a bag of fertiliser.

"Four hundred and ten," she said.

"And how much do you have to pay?"

It was difficult to convince Ngombians that the price of anything was what you had to pay for it, and not what Filosofa decreed.

"One thousand eight hundred," she said.

Two days later I asked her whether she had bought her

fertiliser. She looked sheepish and said nothing. I asked again, and she told me the fertiliser had been sold out by the time she reached the co-operative store. And the money? She had used it to buy a pair of fur-lined boots, a charitable donation from Northern Europe that had found its way to Mbaba market. At first, I was inclined to anger, but soon I laughed at her innocence and guilelessness. She laughed too. How could I remain angry with her?

Athena derived such pleasure from small gifts that I wondered whether it was not worth a life of deprivation to experience it. When I returned from a short business trip to Europe, I brought her back a set of the stereophonic headphones that are the new beads of Africa. She grasped them in her hands, hardly daring to believe they were hers; she squealed with delight. Her voice vibrated with heartfelt gratitude whenever she spoke to me for the next three weeks. The first day she walked about in a daze of delight, the second, with the headphones rendering her oblivious of the rest of the world. By the third day the batteries were completely dead, and she asked for more. I told her to use them more sparingly, for they were very difficult to find in Ngombia. Thenceforth, she was never without her headphones, whether she had batteries or not; and even when they were silent, she walked through the village wearing them, her head thrown back proudly, savouring the envious stares of the villagers.

Occasionally my wife sent me small parcels of delicacies with visitors to the plantation. I let Athena try them all. She was not greatly impressed by smoked salmon or asparagus but took to chocolate truffles as though she intended them to become her staple. The treat at the Christmas party given by the church to the children of Mbaba was a slice of dry bread and tea with sugar in it; and Athena, for whom sugar was an almost inconceivable luxury, had never imagined there was anything so delicious in the world as truffles. When she ate one, her face melted involuntarily into an expression of joy so great that she might have been a mystic in sudden contact with the Ineffable. The box of truffles exerted a powerful magnetic effect on her fingers, and she resorted to all the petty subterfuges – rearranging the remaining chocolates, removing them from the second layer first – that I remembered employing as a child in similar circumstances.

It was some time before I realised that Athena had taken up with the garden boy, Elastic. He was charming, with a ready grin that revealed a veritable keyboard of beautiful white teeth. He was thin but broad-shouldered and muscular, and his limbs were very supple. His understanding of English was also supple, varying from day to day and even from moment to moment, depending on whether he wished to understand what was being said to him. His intelligence was likewise changeable.

Elastic was something of an *homme fatal*: the village was littered with his offspring, so one heard. I knew from the first that he was not entirely honest, but it took me some time to uncover the full extent of his dishonesty. I blamed myself then for having been so naive as to like him. For a long time, his smile camouflaged his thefts, but eventually I came to realise that I was running short of clothes. Someone must have taken them, and Elastic was the prime suspect. At first, I was reluctant to make enquiries, lest a question be taken for an accusation, but this delicacy of feeling soon reduced me to a mere three pairs of socks, when I had arrived with more than twenty. I asked Athena whether she had any idea where they had gone, and she replied that they had disappeared from the washing line. I asked her why she had not mentioned it, and she looked at her toes and mumbled that she was afraid of being dismissed. My assurance that I had not for a moment suspected her only partly comforted her.

My long delay in adverting to the thefts, however, only convinced Elastic they had gone undetected, and he grew careless. One day he appeared at work wearing a shirt I recognised as my own. He said he bought it at Mbaba market. But on his face I saw – not guilt, exactly, but alarm. I took him aside to where we should not be overheard – more delicacy of feeling.

"Don't be a fool, Elastic," I said. "If you must steal, steal only a little at a time. If you steal everything you can lay your hands on, you're bound to be caught."

He claimed not to have understood what I said, but his face told me otherwise. I promised to overlook his crimes if he returned everything he had stolen, and when he did, I stood amazed at the extent of his robbery. Oddly enough, I felt a kind of gratitude to him for having returned my own property. Becoming maudlin, like a drunk, I even rewarded him by giving some of it back, having convinced myself – fatal reasoning! – that his need was greater than mine.

It never took long for Elastic to recover his habitual jauntiness. Within two weeks he asked me for an increase in wages which I had promised him some time before.

"It was on condition your service was satisfactory," I said.

Elastic did not understand.

"You promise more money," he repeated.

"Provided you were satisfactory," I repeated in my turn. "You can hardly call it satisfactory when you steal all my clothes."

"I not understanding," he said doggedly.

"You understand well enough."

"No, no," he said, shaking his head in vehement denial and rolling his eyes. "No, no understand."

When I laughed at his performance he was offended, for he had begun to believe in it himself.

He laid a kind of siege to me. Hardly a day passed when he did not ask about his increased wages. He had an air almost of grievance about him: he had understood the promise but not, apparently, the condition attached. Finally, I gave in and granted him his increase, adding that he must not steal from me for at least six months.

"No, no, never," he said, his comprehension miraculously restored.

I made excuses to myself for him. He must have considered me a man of infinite wealth, able to replace easily anything I lost. For him to steal from me, therefore, was small crime. In fact, it was his contribution to what Filosofa called 'the necessary profound redistribution of the world's resources'.

I first learnt of his affair with Athena when I stumbled across them one day whispering together in an intimate way. It is odd that it should have surprised me: perhaps it had not occurred to me that either of them had a private life or secrets of their own. Like a young child who cannot grasp the continued existence of an object after it has disappeared from his view, I thought that once Athena and Elastic had finished their day's work, they ceased to live.

In fact, their affair came to consume more and more of their working time; they engaged in long and tortuous whispered discussions on the verandah, from which Athena emerged either smiling or crying. Her work, never performed at a furious pace, was now seriously slowed down. Elastic began to neglect the garden. At first, I said nothing, but eventually I spoke to Athena. To my surprise, she opened her heart to me, insofar as her fragmented English and my fragmented Ngijwi made it possible. Elastic now lived with her, she said, though she knew he was not a good man. Still, her children needed a father and besides... It was clear that despite his faults, she harboured something like a passion for him. He took her money, he drank too much, he helped neither in the fields nor in the home, he was unreliable and unfaithful, and sometimes he beat her. It sounded like a recipe for utter misery, at least on her part. I sympathised but told her that all the same she must do her work. She took this as a reproach, the first I had ever given her; she curtsied and in a little while I heard her sobbing gently in the kitchen. A truffle restored a wan smile to her face.

Nevertheless, matters did not improve: in fact, they deteriorated. Their whispered conversations grew more heated, developing into full-blown shouting matches, cut suddenly and unnaturally short by my appearance on the scene. I had never imagined that people so close to subsistence could spare the energy for exhausting emotional entanglements, but so it proved to be. I resolved to intervene once more.

Before I could do so, however, there was a crisis. Athena

arrived one morning in a state of tearful terror. Her story was not coherent, but I managed to piece it together. Two days previously she had told Elastic that she never wanted to see him again (except unavoidably at work), and he must therefore quit her hut. At first Elastic had pleaded with her, but she had remained adamant. Elastic's manhood having been affronted, he swore revenge. Now his revenge had come.

He had left her hut as she demanded but had returned in the night while she was asleep and planted some stolen furniture and a can of diesel amongst her maize. (The theft of diesel was classified as *sabotage* in Ngombia.) In the morning, Elastic had gone to the police to report that he had found stolen goods on Athena's land, and now the police were coming to arrest her.

How she was informed of the intentions of the police I do not know. The bush telegraph was a highly efficient instrument. But without delay I drove to the police station with her, where I explained very forcefully that it was preposterous to suppose that Athena was a thief, that the goods were obviously part of a plot to frame her, and that therefore the police could not possibly arrest her. They were so surprised that a white man was testifying that a black was not a thief that they at once abandoned all plans to arrest Athena.

I should, of course, have fired Elastic at once, for he had shown a vicious and vindictive side to his character. But I was reluctant to dismiss him because I was still sentimental enough to make allowances for him, besides which I assumed (wrongly, as it transpired) that dismissal would have dire personal consequences for him. I contented myself with merely warning him not to behave in such a way again. At first, he denied that he had done it, but then said he had acted out of frustrated passion.

Elastic had decided in any case that his days in my employ were numbered, and that he might as well be fired for a sheep as a lamb. When I came home one afternoon earlier than usual, I found him secreting garden tools in some long grass at the far end of the garden, for collection and removal after dark. He also had there a cache of plates, saucepans, bedclothes, soap and other household items. His attitude on being caught was not of guilt or even embarrassment, but of mild irritation at such ill-luck. This time I fired him at once, without torturing myself with reflections on his poverty and hard life. He made only very feeble attempts on this occasion to excuse himself, saying that he was secreting the tools there for later use in that part of the garden, and that he wanted only to borrow them for use in Athena's fields, where he had never been known to work before. As to the saucepans and so forth, it was a complete mystery to him how they got there. I did not relent: I gave him his remaining wages and told him he was indeed fortunate not to be handed over to the police.

I expected Athena to rejoice that I had dismissed Elastic. But she predicted only trouble in it for her. He would believe it was she who had informed on him, she said, and had led me to catch him red-handed. She awaited his revenge in great fear.

It was not long in coming. Next day, while she was out at work, Elastic went to her hut and, in full view of her children who, however, were too small to stop him, cleared it of all her possessions, down to the pictures on the walls. He found her small money savings in a tin and took them too. When Athena told me next day, she had already gone to the police, but they were indifferent for she had nothing left with which to bribe them to take an interest in her case except herself, and she had surprised them by saying she was *not* a prostitute.

Once more we went to the police station together. Our appearances there were becoming regular. The two policemen were playing cards and took the view that crime was none of their concern. After all, if they went round arresting everyone in Ngombia who had committed a crime, there would soon be no-one left at liberty, and no time for cards either. They asked me what I expected them to do.

"Search for Elastic and arrest him, of course," I said.

Something in my voice told them I was not to be trifled with and reluctantly – after slowly pulling on their decrepit boots – they went to search for him.

I suspected that Elastic would by now be trying to leave the village, and sure enough he was found at the roadside, waiting for a lift. The police arrested him. He took this fresh reverse with impressive calm. If there had been a truck out of Mbaba only ten minutes earlier, he would have got away. He had nothing to be ashamed of, therefore.

The case came up before the magistrate, the successor to Mr Brown, who in the meantime had been appointed to high judicial office. For the sake of the company, and by means of whisky, I had attained a certain influence over the new magistrate. He knew that I expected a conviction and a pretty stiff sentence. Still, twelve years' hard labour seemed excessive: I found it hard to conceive of Elastic as anything worse than a complete rogue. But the new magistrate said he was going to stamp out un-Mutualist behaviour in Mbaba, following the illustrious example of Mr Brown. He asked me afterwards whether I was satisfied with twelve years, obviously expecting an extra reward for his severity. He was disturbed to hear that I thought his sentence – well, over-zealous.

"No, no," he said. "One cannot be too severe on these hooligans and wreckers."

So Elastic was led away to serve his sentence. For a time, he was a little on my conscience. Whenever the sun was particularly fierce, I thought of him breaking stones, or whatever Ngombian hard labour prescribed. Eventually, I convinced myself he deserved his fate.

I need not have worried. A few weeks later, a shadow fell across my desk as I was working. I looked up. In front of me was a man dressed in the light khaki uniform of the Ngombian police. Preoccupied with my work as I was, it took me a few moments to make out that it was none other than Elastic. Somehow, he had managed to get himself out of gaol and into the police.

"Elastic!" I exclaimed.

"Ssh!" he said, putting his index finger to his lips. "Not Elastic now. Boniface."

He gave me the grin that had once all but taken me in. He had come just to say hello, he said, to give me his greetings as he passed through Mbaba. He harboured no grudge against me. He accepted that we had both done what we had both had to do.

Elastic-Boniface left my office. What should I have felt? Outrage, amusement, irritation, contempt, affection, sadness, admiration, anger, resignation? I didn't know then, and I don't know now.

OUT OF AFRICA & THESIS X

Human Mutualism is not a doctrine only for Ngombia. It is valid for all nations.

Filosofa Cicero B. Nyayaya

I returned home as I had planned, to my work and suburban existence. Outwardly, nothing had changed, but often I found myself, against my will, thinking of Ngombia. The village and its people, the sunset over the blue-green hills, the sour smell of fermenting bamboo juice, the sound of Father Ordoñez's voice propounding a fierce truth, came back to me with almost hallucinatory force. But I was unsure whether or not I longed to return to Africa: home had its compensations.

I scanned the newspapers for items about Ngombia, but such as there were conveyed no more of the country's reality than a railway timetable conveys the atmosphere of a busy station. Then one day I noticed a small public announcement: to celebrate the twenty-fifth anniversary of the signing of Filosofa's Harisha Declaration, the International Federation for Peace and Friendship was sponsoring a public lecture to be given by Bishop Herbalgoode, the famous pacifist priest who befriended Filosofa in the days shortly before independence. It was said that the Bishop was still one of Filosofa's spiritual advisers, and he travelled frequently to Ngombia from his slum diocese to console Filosofa for the travails of power.

I went to the meeting. It was held in a hall of the university; the audience of sixty was deeply intellectual, to judge from its mode of dress. I arrived just as the Bishop rose on the platform to speak. He was a tall man in a simple soutane, tied in the middle with an old brown leather belt. His hair was a sleek and distinguished silver, his handsome face surprisingly unlined by his years of deep concern for the unfortunate of the world. His back was ramrod straight; it was not easy to believe he was seventy years old. He spoke with a clarity bordering on the pedantic.

He recalled with affection his first encounter with Filosofa. It was on the wooden verandah of his modest two-room house in Ndinji. The date of independence had been set, and Filosofa was to be Ngombia's first Prime Minister. He greeted Father Herbalgoode (he wasn't a bishop yet) shyly, hardly daring to look him in the eye. Conversation at first was not easy; but when they started to discuss the political meaning of the Gospel, they quickly found common ground, and all restraint fell away. Filosofa returned indoors to fetch the poem he had written only that morning:

Now we are free and sovereign
What am I to do with this nation?
I lie awake and cannot sleep:
Sometimes I think I am too young.

It was so typical of Filosofa's modesty, the Bishop said, that he himself should openly have questioned his ability to lead at a time when no-one else entertained such doubts.

The Bishop continued by describing the enthusiasm that the Harisha Declaration aroused in Ngombia, especially among the idealistic students of the time. They offered to go to the countryside during their vacations to help with the harvest: now that the land belonged to the people, they said, it was the duty of every citizen to develop new forms of production for the benefit of all.

I won't repeat everything the Bishop said: he spoke for more than an hour. He ended on a philosophical note, analysing the roots of Filosofa's ideas. First, there was his appreciation of the value of science and technology, which so far in history had been used only to oppress the people further, but which, when socially controlled, was a force for their liberation. Then, more importantly, was the traditional solidarity of African village society, in which decisions were taken communally and by consensus, in which everyone was equal and no-one was left by the wayside. Finally, and most importantly, there was the Gospel, with its call to charity, fraternity and universal love. Filosofa's government had taken up the challenge to institutionalise the teachings of Christ, who had always been on the side of the poor and the oppressed. Human Mutualism was the doctrine that reconciled all these influences and, in a world still thirsting for a New Beginning, Filosofa's ideas stood as a beacon in the night.

www.ingramcontent.com/pod-product-compliance
Lightning Source LLC
Chambersburg PA
CBHW051951170626
46808CB00007B/2562